Sentimental Journey

by Patti Hales

Over the years they'd drifted apart. So the last thing she needed now was a stroll down memory lane . . .

N ICE day for it," Clive says, and Ellie nods vaguely. She accepts the cup of coffee he's holding out to her. Turning away, she stares bleakly out of the kitchen window.

A nice day for it, he says.

Ellie bites her lower lip and concentrates on the sky, partly because it's there, but mostly because she knows that if she allows herself to be drawn into a discussion, she'll end up blurting out that she doesn't want to go. That maybe they should just stay at home and talk about whether they should carry on like this, or if it would be better ⟨for both⟩ of them to go their separate ways.

Sunlight flows into the room and warms her face through the glass. The sky is filled with the promise of a wonderful spring day.

That fact alone fills Ellie with desolation, pain even.

She thinks she might feel better if it was raining, with heavy grey clouds to match her mood.

When something's over, it's over. Life will never be the same again for Clive and her. She thinks it's called the point of no return, but she's actually reluctant to say the words, "Enough is enough".

It's no-one's fault, she tells herself. It's just circumstances.

We've become typical victims of the work ethnic of our time.

Often she thinks about Clive, usually in the middle of a busy day. His face swims into her mind . . . his thick brown hair, gentle grey eyes and very kissable mouth.

Sometimes her hand reaches out for the phone. Then she stops. He's probably tied up. Interruptions are the last thing he wants. Of course she'll talk to him later, she always thinks.

But she never does. For all kinds of reasons.

Only a couple of weeks ago, in a rare moment of closeness, Clive had admitted to doing exactly the same thing and thinking exactly the same thoughts, leaving Ellie feeling that both of them seemed to spend a lot of time thinking, but never actually doing.

YOU'RE miles away," Clive says. Ellie wishes she was miles away and that Clive had at least consulted her before going ahead and planning a day out. Especially on a Sunday.

It's the one day of the week she can call her own. The one when she has time to read the papers and take a long, lazy bath.

And Sundays, for Clive, usually mean a trip down to the local for a lunch-time drink with his friends.

For both of them, it's a day to recharge tired batteries — but not together.

A further wave of fury scorches Ellie at the unfairness of losing her precious Sunday.

If she knew where they were heading, it might not be so bad, but when she'd asked Clive, he'd just smiled.

"You'll understand when we get there," was all he'd said, leaving her feeling vulnerable and remembering the time when there were no secrets between them.

She remembers the early years, the constant struggle to pay the mortgage on their first tiny flat. Clive had been in his final year at college and she'd been a lowly Girl Friday.

Juggling their finances to pay all the bills and eat had been one long, delicious struggle.

She'd hurled a whole plate of spaghetti bolognaise at him once.

He'd ducked and they'd had to repaint the dining-room wall to get rid of the orange stain.

They'd eventually fallen into bed, exhausted and giggling.

But together. Very, very together.

E LLIE?" Clive gently removes the coffee cup from her hand, and prises her tense fingers from the handle.

"Your car or mine?" she asks flatly.

"Bus." He smiles as her mouth drops open. Carefully, he places one finger under her chin and raises her lower jaw. For a moment, she wonders if he's going to kiss her or if she should kiss him. Then the moment is gone.

"Bus," Ellie repeats weakly, grabbing her jacket and bag.

And sitting on the top deck she struggles to remember the last time they used public transport. A very long time ago, she suspects. When they'd been poverty-stricken newly-weds.

Strange how they'd thought then that money would solve all their problems; a big detached house and foreign holidays to exotic locations would prove that they'd really "made it".

Her spirits perk up as the bus pulls up outside the mainline station. Clive's arm is firm under her elbow as he helps her off then dashes into the ticket office.

As she waits, childhood memories engulf her, cosset her into a cocoon of anticipation. Two weeks at the seaside, armed with a bucket, spade and shrimp net. And new sandals, always new sandals, red leather ones with a cut-out pattern on the toes.

Engrossed in the electronic time-table, Clive seems to have forgotten he's not alone. Ellie feels helpless. He used to pick up her thoughts. As her eyes narrow, he spins round and grabs her hand.

"We've got two minutes. Run!"

Together they race along the grubby concrete. "This will do." Clive pushes her through the narrow door on to the waiting train. He spends several moments deciding where they'll sit . . . as if it really matters, Ellie thinks . . . then he nudges her into a seat by the window and flops down opposite her.

"Will I be wasting my breath if I ask where we're going?"

"Does it really matter where? Isn't it just being together that's supposed to count?" Was that just the tiniest hint of accusation?

Ellie's throat tightens as the train pulls out of the station.

"Margate," he says suddenly.

"Eh?" She's sure she's misheard what he's telling her. They're not Margate kind of people any more. Maybe once, but not now . . .

"We're going to Margate. To play at being day-trippers."

She feels like letting her tears flow.

"Listen to me." Clive sounds as though he's talking through a long tunnel. "We were happy in Margate. We scrimped and saved for weeks. Lunch was greasy hotdogs, then we sat on the beach and shared a candy-floss, a big, multi-coloured one on a stick."

He stops for a moment, then: "I won that mouldy-looking teddy-bear with the crossed eyes. We stared at the pier that wasn't there any more, we ran away before the man could collect the money for the deck-chairs we'd only sat in for five minutes, and we laughed all day."

His eyes fix on a point above her head. "We never laugh any more, Ellie, do we?"

Ellie's mind focuses on the teddy-bear stuck on top of the wardrobe in one of the spare bedrooms. It must be the bear's seventh birthday . . .

To her amazement, she remembers the day vividly. Not only remembers, but sees it in glorious Technicolor.

"We bought silly hats," she begins slowly, then the words begin to tumble out. "We went to the funfair . . . you cuddled me when I screamed on the ghost train and we paddled in the sea as the sun went down." A smile breaks out on her tired face. "You told me to listen for the hiss when it hit the water. And I believed you. I really listened."

Clive nods thoughtfully. Relief softens his set features.

"We had a wonderful time, didn't we?"

"Wonderful," Ellie confirms, and as the train slows into the station she springs to her feet. Reaching out, she entwines her fingers through Clive's and pulls him to his feet.

On the seafront, she pulls the restricting clasp from her long blonde hair and lets the gentle breeze toss it around.

It's all there . . . the salty tang, the candy-floss, the smell of the funfair. Young lovers saunter, hand in hand, oblivious to everything except each other. Exactly as it had been before for them.

A whoop of joy escapes from her lips. On tiptoe, she kisses Clive's smooth cheek, then his mouth, shuddering in delight as his arms tighten round her as if he'll never let her go again.

"I love you, Ellie." His voice caresses her.

The sweetest words in the world.

"I love you, too," she tells him. "I've never stopped loving you."

"No." His fingers placed gently on her lips stop her and Ellie nods.

How close they nearly came, she thinks as she snuggles against his chest. How horribly easy to become careless. How fragile is this thing called love.

Margate . . . good old Margate on a Sunday in spring, and Ellie's sprits soar as high as the big wheel turning slowly over their heads.■

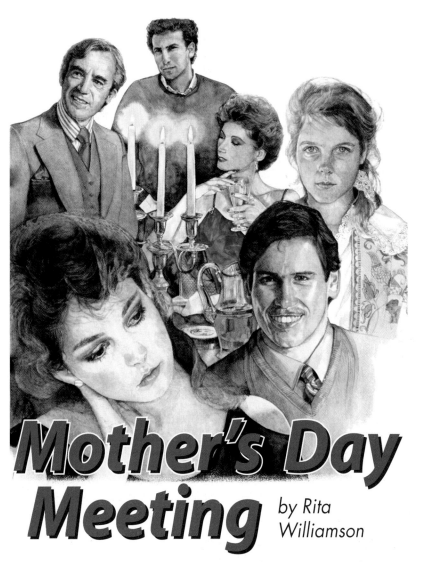

Mother's Day Meeting

by Rita Williamson

This year, more than all our expensive presents, what she really needed was our blessing . . .

IT'S Mother's Day. Well, actually, it's the day before — Saturday evening — and we're celebrating the event slightly in advance. When I say "we", I mean my husband's family. My own family's approach to this celebration is quite, quite different.

When Mum was alive, we all turned up on the actual day and spoiled her rotten with chocolates and our exuberance.

This family prefers a small dinner in a smart restaurant.

It wouldn't have suited my mum. In fact, it doesn't suit me. But it seems right for Bob's mother, Davinia.

I hope I don't sound bitter or at odds with the Westerleys, because that wouldn't be true. I'm very happy being Mrs Bob Westerley — it's just that I recognise the differences between us.

Even though Bob and I have been married for years (very happily, too, before you wonder) and I've come to accept that the Westerleys are more reserved than we are, I still find it hard coming to terms with their ways.

In my family, we celebrated Mother's Day with boxes of chocolates and still-sticky cards which the little kids had made specially.

For Davinia, we present elegant gifts, beautifully-wrapped, along with framed photographs of all the children.

This morning, my own three woke me with tea and cornflakes in bed.

They also joined me in it, to unwrap my presents: a box of jelly beans, a pair of new slippers and a "Thank You" card from the pets.

I was impressed by the ingenuity needed to get the hamster's paw-prints on the card. Conversely, I thought that little effort would have been required to get Scruffy the dog's "signature" — he leaves paw-prints everywhere.

And Bob? For starters, he gave me a dozen red roses and a luscious kiss, and he promised further gifts in our hotel room.

For, you see, tonight we're staying at the smart hotel of which this upmarket restaurant is a part, just the two of us — and the rest of Bob's family.

It's the first and last time I intend to be away from my children on Mother's Day.

Davinia, who organised the whole thing, had promised us a surprise, and she wasn't joking. In fact, maybe bombshell would be a better description.

This family is reeling, and the reason is Cameron Thraves, Davinia's new husband-to-be. Charles, her first husband, died about six or seven years ago, but this appears not to be a sufficiently respectful mourning period as far as her children are concerned.

For the first time in a long while, these children with their disparate lives are united. I begin to feel for Davinia.

It's no wonder Davinia has found another man. She's still startlingly attractive, and has the vivacity of a 35-year-old, not someone who's just shy of her 53rd birthday.

Cameron, her beau, seems to suit her. He's large, ebullient and positively lights up when she speaks or moves.

Davinia made her shock announcement prior to the meal, and now we're lingering over cheese and biscuits, sipping port and listening to her telling us about Cameron.

He's a writer, an ex-journalist who has used his knowledge (and no doubt his contacts) to write thrillers on corporate espionage. His books appear frequently in the shops, if not on the best-seller lists.

Tim and Helen are enthusiastic, as always. Helen, the baby of Davinia's three children, is a university lecturer and is married to a professor of English literature.

"Gosh, Cameron," they chime together, "how exciting!"

With his almost manic enthusiasm for pure literature, Tim quizzes Cameron on the value of the 20th-century novel as a printed art form.

I catch a flash of annoyance on Davinia's face, but Cameron takes it all in his stride.

"I don't pretend to be something I'm not, Tim.

"I just like writing old-fashioned spy stories."

Farther down the table is Peter. Peter's unmarried and, frankly, I'm not surprised. His finicky ways and ingrained bachelor habits would try the patience of a saint.

Apart from that, he's the most clichéd of accountants, whose idea of a fun night out is to sit at his computer and calculate the monthly profit of his financial consultancy.

Peter almost attacks Cameron with the strength of his own concerns.

What does Cameron earn from his writing?

Does he write off travel against tax?

How has he invested his royalties?

Davinia wriggles uneasily on her chair. She's obviously proud of Peter's expert knowledge, yet concerned about how Cameron will take this savage grilling about his "prospects".

Cameron listens stoically, then, when he's had enough, he settles for a gentle rebuke.

"I don't bother with all that," he says. "That's what I pay my accountant for . . ."

Peter is put quietly but firmly in his place.

I think I like Cameron!

He returns his complete attention to Davinia and soothes away the frown that's beginning to settle on her face. It's easy to see that he loves her.

Beside me, my husband's feelings radiate like heat. I can sense his shock and can almost hear his emotions struggling to come to terms with it all.

He has worried about his mother often. Our blissful togetherness seemed to emphasise her loneliness. Now, faced with Davinia choosing a new partner, he's less sure.

Poor Davinia. All her children are rigid with shock instead of bouncing with joy.

The talk babbles on, the inquisition continues, and the mood becomes clearer. These cuckoos do not want another bird in their nest. Underneath the charm and the wit, I can feel the undercurrent of rejection.

I nudge Bob, and with a nod of my head, make him observe the tender looks exchanged between his mother and Cameron.

His face softens as he recognises them for love. He swallows down his resentment and smiles at me.

"He'll be good for her, won't he?" he whispers into my ear, and I nod back.

Already Cameron's charm and care have put the smile back on Davinia's face. I just wish her children could see past their own prejudice to what is really important here.

Poor Davinia. I wonder, for a moment, if she regrets bringing her children up to be so polite and reserved.

I know that my family would have handled this better. We'd have been shocked, I suppose, but I don't think we'd have closed ranks, like Bob's family.

THEN suddenly I realise that this is my family, too, and I'm letting it happen! I'm appalled. My mother would be ashamed of me. She taught me better than this.

She'd tell me that, instead of bleating on about their bad behaviour, I should be showing them a good example.

I realise that my complaints cut both ways. Maybe they haven't wholly accepted me, but I've not given much of myself either. They've split us into two families, but I've let them.

I grit my teeth. I know how it feels to be shut out of this family and I won't let them do it to Cameron.

I look again at Davinia's face as she hopes for a positive sign from her children. Their blessing means so much to her, she'll beg for it soon.

But she shouldn't have to. It's almost Mother's Day. They should give her this gift gladly.

"I'd like to make a toast." Every head turns in my direction as I rise to my feet. It's not often that I have much to say at these affairs, let alone make a spectacle of myself.

I ignore my peers and turn to my mother-in-law and the man beside her.

"Perhaps I'm not the best person to be doing this, but I want to be the first!" My voice is slightly shaky. "I'd just like to welcome Cameron to the family."

A wave of shock rolls around the table at my effrontery and I share a smile of daring with Davinia.

I turn my attention to the object of my speech. "I joined this family six years ago when I married Bob and I want to tell you how kind and welcoming everyone is."

Here, I have his full attention and hope he doesn't recognise fiction when he hears it.

"I know they'll all take you to their hearts, Cameron." I glance around the table to make it clear that this is an order. "Especially since you make Davinia so happy. We're delighted for you both."

I pause. Should I go on? Why not! I might as well be hung for a sheep as a lamb.

"I'd also like to say how indebted I am to Cameron for so many hours of enthralling and pleasurable entertainment. I love your books and look forward to badgering you to write the next one!"

There, I'd said it! No snobbery, no patronising condescension, just honest appreciation.

"Hear, hear!" Bob echoes my sentiments and Davinia glows at me like a jewel.

"Now, please," I say, in the tone of voice I use to settle childish disputes at home, "let's raise our glasses and drink to Davinia and Cameron."

We all drink, and I can see the shine of happy tears in Davinia's eyes. I feel Bob squeeze my hand and I blurt out the invitation I'm sure he wanted to issue.

"We'd like you both to come to dinner tomorrow. The kids'll go wild when they hear about Grandma!"

I can feel the surprise from around the table, but I ignore it and look at Davinia.

She smiles at me, and I know that after all these years, she and I have come to an understanding.

I feel like taking a risk with this new relationship.

"Come on, Davina. Come to the madhouse and let us spoil you both for
a day."

She smiles at me and takes Cameron's hand.

"You know," she says, "I think we'd really love that!" ∎

This Old House

by D.L. Garrard

Most buyers would want to turn it into a comfortable family home. Richard, however, wanted to turn it into a quick profit!

"OH, no!" Richard groaned. He stood on the dusty doorstep of his new home and rummaged through his pockets for the third time. No key!

"Unbelievable!" he shouted theatrically.

A breathless voice behind him said, "Excuse me, have you seen my cat?"

Richard spun round to see a young woman with wind-blown fair hair propping up an ancient bicycle.

"No — why should I have?" he demanded, acutely embarrassed lest she'd witnessed his childish outburst. "I've hardly been here for five minutes!"

"I know," she said. "You see," "he used to live here with Miss Quilley and now he's gone missing. I just thought he might be sitting on your doorstep.

"He's called Snowy, and I'm Jess Holroyd, by the way.

"I'll give you my number."

She scribbled a number on the back of a supermarket receipt

which he stuffed into the pocket of his jeans and forgot almost before she'd pedalled away.

He'd been advised that he should replace all the existing doors and windows for added security — yet the loss of a key was quite sufficient to keep out a law-abiding owner!

HE broke a kitchen window, climbed in onto the window-seat — and stepped on a cat. It screeched and ran across the room. It was a large, black creature.

Obviously it had come through the cat flap, the catch of which, like everything else, was in disrepair. Actually, the state of the property was what had made it so temptingly low in price.

The cat went, but not without a haughty stare. It had a limp, its tail was half missing, its right ear tattered.

Richard knew nothing about cats. When he'd climbed the professional ladder and could afford the classy country home he envisaged, he would have a dog. He rather fancied a red setter, though his future wife (brunette or redhead, tall and elegant) would have a say, of course.

He unlatched the front door and began to unload his belongings.

The hazy sun was setting beyond the row of beeches which faced the house. Beech Lodge stood a short way down the avenue, which turned off the main road that ran through the village, and was exactly what Richard had been looking for.

As he dragged the last but one box from the van, the door key tinkled to the ground.

Feeling more than a little jaded by now, he stepped uncertainly into the still-unfamiliar surroundings, and remembered forlornly about the broken window pane.

Wearily, he fixed it temporarily with cardboard and sticky tape, then took himself off to the Westerhill Arms — and a scrumptious supper.

NEXT morning, he was on his way to return the van and collect his car before he remembered, with a twinge of guilt, that he still hadn't rung about the cat.

But he'd changed out of his dirty jeans and so he didn't have Jess's phone number with him.

He put it out of his mind and let recent events scroll through it instead, in an orderly fashion.

Having gained promotion, he'd decided to buy a house which he could improve and sell at a profit.

The proposed bypass beyond the avenue would be a useful selling point.

Later, when he drove back into the avenue, the evening sky had a luminosity which threw Beech Lodge into relief. He walked up the path with a feeling of homecoming which surprised him.

His mind on fitted kitchens — though that would have to wait a while — he went through with his carrier bags. The cat was back on the window-seat.

Richard found the scrap of paper and his mobile phone.

"Hello?" The answering voice was warm, with a slight huskiness, putting Richard suddenly in mind of candlelight and wine and elegant feminine company.

"Hello . . . sorry to trouble you. My name's Richard Felsham, I'm ringing about a missing cat . . . Jess Holroyd told me to ring here if —"

The voice became excited and familiar, shattering his dreamy vision.

"Oh, great! You've found him? This is Jess speaking," she added.

"Oh, right!" Richard was taken aback. "Yes, your cat was inside all the time. He must have gone through the cat flap. Shall I bring him round?"

"Well . . . if you wouldn't mind . . . I live at 6A Park Crescent, Beckerston."

He found a cardboard box, and advanced cautiously on the cat.

He stalked it towards the open car door, and when it stretched up to investigate, he swiftly assisted it inside.

WITH the aid of a street map, he located No. 6 Park Crescent, aware of the cat's flickering eyes on his back.

Jess Holroyd was watching for him. She ran down the path bright-eyed and eager, then drew back sharply.

"Oh! But that's not Snowy!" she cried.

His jaw dropped. "But it must be!"

"D'you think I don't know my own cat?"

"Well, this one was inside making itself at home yesterday, and again today . . ."

"Yesterday?" she said sharply. "And you waited till now before —?"

"But if it really isn't your cat —"

"That's not the point! And for goodness' sake," she exclaimed, "who'd call a black cat Snowy?"

"But you never told me its name!" he argued.

"Oh, I'm sorry. It's just that I'm very upset about losing Snowy."

"I'm sorry for yelling at you," he apologised. "But I'm not used to cats, you see.

"I suppose you couldn't take this one, till his new owner turns up?" he appealed. She looked at him in a way which made him feel lacking, somehow. Her grey-green eyes were decidedly unfriendly.

"Rusty — that's what Miss Quilley named the cat you've got there — is a stray, by choice. He wouldn't let you, me, Miss Quilley, or anyone else adopt him.

"He'd only have used the cat flap because the house was empty. He fends for himself in the woods, so you don't need to feel responsible."

Up until now, he'd prided himself on his easy rapport with the opposite sex, but he felt completely out of his depth here.

"Well, I hope Snowy turns up safe and well." It was all he could think of to say.

Then he drove Rusty back to Beech Lodge, where he let him out into the darkness and went to make himself a snack.

The house seemed depressingly quiet. The kitchen was the cosiest place, with its solid fuel stove, window seats and a scratched but sturdy captain's chair. Good enough to restore, he noted.

The sudden clatter of the cat flap startled him.

Rusty peered through it, then stepped in. A pink tongue licked black whiskers at the pervading smell of sardines on toast.

With childish satisfaction, after what Jess had said, Richard opened another can on to an old plate and put down a saucer of milk. The cat padded over, tasted the fish, sniffed the milk critically, gave a bored yawn and went out through the flap once more.

Richard laughed aloud.

"OK — you can have the last word!"

WITH double glazing and new doors in place, Richard set to work in the lounge. He uncovered a beautiful, open marble fireplace which had been boarded up.

A few coats of pale emulsion worked wonders. Soon the room looked so much more spacious light, fresh and clean.

He went into Beckerston and bought curtains in rich, warm colours, and a couple of rugs to lay on the freshly-varnished floorboards. He took a fancy, too, to an enormous tweedy chair that practically held out its arms and begged to be taken home.

In genuine bewilderment, he looked at it later, squatting by the fireplace. It was deep and squashy and big enough to seat two!

He got started on his bedroom. Opening the window, he spotted Rusty stalking through the undergrowth.

Later, when he opened the back door to put out some rubbish, a dead fieldmouse lay on the doorstep. Rusty was sitting on the nearby fence.

"What's this? A peace offering?" "Or an entrance ticket?"

Intrigued, he left the door ajar.

When he came downstairs to eat, Rusty was surveying the kitchen from the window seat as if he owned the place.

After eating, Richard went upstairs to add a few finishing touches to the bedroom and when he came down again, the cat had vanished.

THE shrill ringing of his new doorbell startled Richard. Jess Holroyd stood on the doorstep, regarding him warily. "Snowy's turned up. Someone took him in. I — I was in the village, so I thought I'd call and let you know . . ." He was absurdly pleased to see her.

"That's great news," he grinned. "Won't you come in for coffee — unless somebody's cat-sitting Snowy and you're in a hurry?"

When she smiled in return, it gave her dimples. "No. No, I'm not." She followed him in. "Oh, this is perfect!" she said approvingly. "I wondered if you'd change it out of all recognition. You know, make it ultra-modern . . ."

"So did I — but things keep getting in the way of my intentions, believe it or not! That kitchen's resisting me, too. It seems to want to keep the old stove. And I heard at the pub that the bypass might be re-routed, thanks to the strong opposition."

She shot him a puzzled glance. "What's the bypass got to do with it?"

"Not as much as I thought it had," Richard replied lightly.

She adamantly refused a lift, but agreed he could walk her to the bus stop. When he opened the door, Rusty ambled in and, purring softly, made straight for the kitchen window seat.

Jess's mouth fell open. "He's purring!"

"We're two of a kind," Richard said solemnly. "And there's more to both of us than meets the eye."

As the bus approached, he said impulsively, "My two oldest friends, Nesta and James, are coming to visit next weekend. So . . . would you consider making up a foursome with us at the Westerhill Arms, for dinner?"

She went pink.

"Well, think about it, Jess. I'll give you a ring later in the week

★★★★

He walked back under the pale March moon and, unlatching the gate, heard a fox bark in the cold, clear air. The sprawling lavender brushed his legs as he went up the path.

That would be a perfume he'd find time to savour, come summer, he thought contentedly. ■

Things would be different now. But it was up to her to show her grandsons that they could still be good...

Everything Changes

by Julie Goodall

THE commotion downstairs was like music to Barbara's ears: the sound of squabbling children. It had been so long since she'd been left alone to deal with something like that.

Smiling for a moment into the mirror, Barbara pulled a comb gently through her grey, loosely-permed hair, then called down the stairs through the open bedroom door. "Are you two ready yet? We'll be going in just a sec."

"Yes, Gran!" her grandsons replied in unison. Silence hovered for a few minutes, until Barbara stood poised at the front door waiting for the boys to thunder down the hall.

"Good! Trainers on . . . Have you got a jumper each in case it gets cold?" Both nodded and pointed to a bag, bulging dangerously at the seams with the bulk of a football.

Dear Linda. Barbara smiled . . . She'd thought of everything and was most probably worrying terribly in case her old widowed mother couldn't cope.

Her heart was in the right place, but if only she'd realised what it was that Barbara had needed during these months since her beloved Daniel had died.

Being wrapped in cotton-wool was not the answer for someone like Barbara Tanton.

She'd needed time alone with her grandchildren — normal time, just as it had been before — but instead Linda had only brought the family to visit all together, unconsciously treating her mother like a delicate china doll.

Or safety in numbers? Perhaps that's what it had been about. No chance then of being drawn into the grief at a more personal level, of having to cope with the real trauma of someone being left alone at the sprightly age of 59.

"Gran? Are you OK?"

Looking up, Barbara realised she had been staring blankly at the carpet, freshly vacuumed for the boys' visit. That had been completely pointless, of course. As if they'd notice something as mundane as a dust-free carpet!

But if Barbara was being honest, she'd admit that it had been a statement to her sweet, misunderstanding daughter. She was trying to say — I'm in control; I'm OK; I can cope.

"I'm fine, Philip. Sorry . . . Phil," she corrected with a grin, pre-empting the sigh which would doubtlessly emerge at her having used his full name.

He was almost twelve now, and had just started at the comprehensive school in the town. To him, full names — like cute baby names — were to be scoffed at. They were simply relics of the past.

Just like his grandpa, Barbara realised with a pang, before opening the front door on to a fresh, sunny afternoon.

THE walk along the clifftop was something the boys had always loved. Barbara and Daniel had lived here all their lives and it was the place where they'd first met.

Although from neighbouring villages, and both hiking fanatics, they'd never actually come across each other until Barbara had twisted her ankle when her foot caught in a rabbit hole one windy morning.

She'd been watching the sea instead of watching where she had been going; a habit she'd never quite managed to kick.

And then Daniel, almost resembling the proverbial knight in shining armour, but carrying a backpack instead of bearing a trusty sword, had come rushing across.

She remembered, even now, the concern etched on his face, and smiled, recalling how she'd put on the agony rather a lot, revelling in the unexpected attention. In the end, he'd insisted on helping her home and she'd hobbled along with her arm around his strong shoulders.

He's always been a soft touch, her Dan, she thought wistfully.

"We're here, Gran!" eight-year-old Simon yelled excitedly. They'd run on ahead, excited in the blustery wind, not having visited the spot since their grandfather had passed away.

Barbara watched as Philip whispered something to his brother, becoming slightly perturbed as the boys just stood, as if not knowing quite what to do.

Throwing them the ball, with the usual warning about not kicking it too near the edge, she sat down on the seat, and settled back to enjoy the breathtaking view for a while.

The sea was fairly calm, with only a few clouds drifting slowly above. The beach was the rich, golden colour of the loveable retriever from up the street, and the water was dotted with surfers attempting to catch the small, intermittent waves.

How many times had she walked along here with Daniel, spreading a rug on the grass and watching the activity below, wishing there had been a bench or a seat to sit on close to the edge of the cliff?

Now, at last, there was, and Barbara read the inscribed words inside her head, not needing to look at the gleaming new plaque stapled to the back of the seat.

For my beloved Daniel, she knew it told all those who rested there, *for the happy times we spent here and the times we will spend here again.*

She knew the family had thought it a disturbing, morbid idea, but one day she hoped they'd understand. It was here that Barbara felt closest to her husband of 33 years — why shouldn't she be the one to provide the seat they'd wanted so much?

SUDDENLY, Barbara became aware of a silence, at once realising that the boys' football game had ceased. They were both watching her, awkward in their stance, as if unsure whether or not to approach their gran.

At once, she knew what was on their minds and cursed her own insensitivity. How selfish she was, for not thinking of how it had been for them, too.

Rising slowly, she watched Simon brush a tear from his small cheek, his eyes downcast, remembering, no doubt, that Grandad had always kicked a ball around with them up here.

"It's not the same without Grandad," Philip muttered, as Barbara bent down and placed an arm around each slim waist.

"No, it won't ever be the same, boys," she agreed with a sigh, knowing full well there was no point in glossing over the truth. The facts hurt, but they had to be faced, even at such a young age.

"It will be different, Phil. But . . ." she said hesitantly. ". . . it can still be all right, love.

"Not perhaps quite as good as when Grandad was here . . ." Her voice faltered. "It'll — it'll just be . . . different," she said again.

"What do you mean?" Simon asked, smearing his face with the back of a grubby hand.

"Well, if you like, I could play with you. I used to play football in the park with the boys when I was a girl," Barbara confided.

"I was good, too, although the boys disallowed half my goals because they knew I was better than them! Now — do you want me in goal, or what?"

Open-mouthed, the boys exchanged glances.

"I want to be in goal first!" Simon announced. "After ten goals, we'll swap."

"OK." And Barbara grinned, withdrawing her comforting arms. "Ten goals! My goodness, it's a long time since I've played football, but I warn you . . . you might be in for a surprise!"

Gently, Barbara took the ball from her grandson and smiled as she placed it on the mutually allocated spot.

An image of Daniel entered her head as she retreated then ran daintily towards it and took a kick.

Into the air flew her slip-on shoe, gliding gracefully before coming to its resting place, just missing the head of a lady who was passing.

Barbara's hand flew to her mouth for a split second, then she dissolved into fits of helpless giggles as she saw identical expressions of horror on the faces of the two shocked boys.

Before long, their laughter could be heard 'way down on the beach.

Things may change, Barbara thought, aware of the happiness and relief she felt inside, but it doesn't mean they can't still be good . . . ■

"We'll Meet Again"

by Sheila Ireland

At least, he hoped they would. Their last meeting, fifty years ago, had been very brief — and completely unforgettable . . .

EVEN as he stood there, high up and windblown, on top of the chalk-faced cliffs, David Haggerty wasn't sure why he had returned to this place.

The 50th anniversary celebrations of VE Day, which had brought him back to England from Canada, were over now.

Old friends, comrades he hadn't seen for many years, had shaken hands, hugged him close, and begun preparations to return to their homes.

Soon, he would have to do the same — but not yet.

There was something else he had to do first.

Now, walking slowly through the long, tufty grass towards the edge of the cliffs and the sea below, David suddenly became aware of an airliner overhead, descending as it came in over the land.

A warm shiver ran down his spine at the sight.

"Laura," he whispered — and all at once he knew he couldn't have left without saying a final farewell to his most precious memory of the summer of 1944.

He remembered he had been returning from a mission over Germany, the controls of the Lancaster juddering in his hands as the aircraft encountered turbulence and crosswinds on its descent.

Up ahead lay the white cliffs of Dover — home base — and a welcome breakfast.

That's when he'd spotted the movement on the cliff top, barely perceptible at first, of a tiny figure, no larger than an ant. Curious, he had altered the rate of his descent, taking the aircraft slowly down, down, down — until he was able to see her quite clearly.

It was a girl in a white dress, on the cliff top, her shiny blonde hair blowing in the wind, her arms stretched upwards, waving a welcome as they approached.

He had never forgotten that heart-stopping moment, David thought now, smiling to himself.

As tired as he was, he had never seen anything so beautiful.

It was as if the weight of war had suddenly been lifted from his shoulders and he had smiled and shaken his head in wonder.

He had tipped his wings in a returning salute.

And he had known, even then, that he just had to see her again.

★★★★

It hadn't been easy, but finally he had been granted a weekend furlough.

He had managed to borrow a car from the base, and had motored down to the cliffs of Dover.

It had been a day much like today, David thought — pale-blue skies, puffs of white cloud and sunlight on the water far below.

The cliff top had been a little windswept then, too — and deserted, just as it was now.

There had been no girl standing there, waving and waiting, as he had somehow imagined there would be.

Of course, he had no right to feel disappointed or let down.

He had just been so incredibly certain she would be there.

He didn't know how long he'd sat there, staring out to sea, the wind blowing in his face.

He didn't know how long it had been before he'd become aware that he was being watched.

All he remembered now was the sudden, warm shiver running down his spine and, when he'd looked around, she had been standing there, smiling.

"Hello," she'd said softly. "You looked as if you were miles away, off in a world of your own."

He'd scrambled to his feet, unable to believe she was really there.

"Just thinking, that's all." He'd returned her smile. "Day-dreaming, I guess."

"You're an American?"

"Canadian."

"Were you thinking about home?" she'd asked.

He'd shaken his head.

"So what do Canadians think about in the middle of a war, sitting on the cliffs of Dover?" she'd asked, smiling at him again.

"The truth?" he'd asked hesitantly.

She'd nodded.

He had looked straight into her eyes then and said, "I was thinking about you . . ."

DAVID stopped walking on the cliffs now. He had reached the place he wanted to be.

He sat down, in exactly the same spot as all those years ago, and he whispered, "Laura, you are very easy to remember . . ."

Laura Davenport.

He had loved her from the very first moment, and had never doubted that she loved him, too.

They had walked together, slowly, on these white cliffs of Dover, and the world had suddenly been at peace.

The happiness had lasted for just a single day, he thought, yet in many ways, it had lasted forever.

In the purple dusk of that summer of '44, they had had tea and scones in the little café in Dover.

They had been very tired and very happy, loving each other because it was impossible to do anything else.

Yet they had both known that it could never be more for them.

"I'm married, David, to a pilot, just like you," Laura had told him .

"The day you saw me waving on the cliffs, I thought it might be Douglas, my husband, flying home from a night-time raid . . ."

"Laura, I —"

"And I have a child, David. A little girl. There — there can never be anything more than today between us."

He could still remember her tears as she stood up.

She'd met his eyes for just a moment. "Goodbye, David. I'll never forget you."

Then she'd run out of the café into the darkening night.

He had never seen her again.

David sighed deeply now.

When the war had finally ended, he hadn't been able to stop himself finding out about Flight Lieutenant Douglas Davenport.

He'd learned that Laura's husband had survived the war and returned home, and so he did the same himself.

In time, of course, he'd met and married his late wife, Anne. Though they'd never had the children they'd hoped for, they'd still had forty very happy years together.

Yet, through all those years, the memories of that unforgettable day with Laura had stayed with him.

He took a slow, lingering look around the clifftop.

"Goodbye, Laura," he whispered softly, turning to leave.

THE little café where they had had tea and scones was gone now, David noticed, replaced by a small fashion boutique.

David wandered slowly through the streets of Dover, not really knowing why he had stopped in the town. Yet, it was peaceful here and he had no real reason to hurry back to the city.

Up ahead, people began filing out of a little church, and David stepped into the churchyard.

The sun was shining, streaming through the leaves of a big oak tree, beyond which he saw the small graveyard.

He walked slowly over, down past the line of headstones, reading the epitaphs and recalling VE Day, the handshakes and hugs of comrades who were going home, the sad thoughts for those who never did.

Suddenly he stopped, feeling almost chilled.

On the headstone in front of him was a dedication to a man he had never known, but whose life had crossed his in a way that could never be forgotten.

In Loving Memory of
DOUGLAS DAVENPORT
Born 5th February, 1920
Died 8th June, 1990.

David sighed deeply and bowed his head.

He didn't, at first, hear a woman enter the churchyard and walk in his direction, carrying a spray of freshly-cut flowers.

Then he noticed her —and felt an incredible feeling of joy sweep over him.

Her hair was no longer blonde but silver-grey and there were lines around her eyes that had not been there before.

Yet she still looked as lovely, as vibrant, as before.

David turned around as the woman saw him, then stopped, staring.

"Laura . . . ?" he whispered. ■

Where Did Our Love Go?

by Joyce Begg

After all these years it was over — and their lives were destined to change forever...

WHEN Geoffrey left Frances, her first reaction had been one of hurt and dismay. She should have seen it coming, of course. The warning signs had all been there.

If Geoffrey said that his trip to Birmingham involved a business dinner, finishing too late for him to come home, then she'd believed him. It hadn't occurred to her to distrust him.

The possibility that the late nights had more to do with his secretary than his workload hadn't entered her mind. They were a happily-married couple, with two grown-up children. They were a unit, a team.

When she'd read the short note he'd left on the kitchen pinboard — like all their other domestic exchanges — the few brief words had sent shock waves through her system.

Frances, the letter ran, I don't know how to say this without hurting you, but I'm leaving.

Pat and I want to be together, so I've taken the lease on a small flat and she's going to move in with me. I'll be in touch about our joint finances. Sorry if this all comes as a bit of a shock.

All best wishes,

Geoffrey.

It was the chill of the last four words that had engulfed her and made her shiver, even on a sunny February afternoon.

Nothing had signified the change between them more dramatically than the intimation that his love had been withdrawn and substituted with his best wishes.

IT was several days before she could admit openly to anyone what had happened. She put off telling the children, not sure how they would react.

Her son, Simon, an accountant with a large London firm, seemed saddened but unsurprised.

"I'm sorry, Mum. If there's anything I can do, just lift the phone."

"Thank you, darling. But you're so busy. There probably isn't much you can do anyway." Except come home, even for the weekend.

There was a lot of Geoffrey in Simon — she had always known that. But she had never before had it quite so clearly demonstrated.

Laura, on the other hand, was a student and as close to a feminist firebrand as any member of their conventional family was likely to get.

"How could he do that! I mean, just dump you, after all these years!"

"That's one way to put it." Frances heard the dryness in her own voice. "Very succinct, darling."

"You know what I mean, Mum. It's typical middle-aged male behaviour.

"Well, he's lost all my respect, I can tell you that! I'll be home tomorrow evening, Mum. See you then. Take care."

Frances smiled ruefully. She questioned how typical Geoffrey's behaviour was. Surely there were thousands of middle-aged men who were happy with their wives, their lives, their middle age in general? What had she done to instigate Geoffrey's betrayal?

"Nothing," her friend and colleague, Margaret, exclaimed when Frances eventually told her what had happened. Margaret was a legal secretary and Frances her part-time assistant.

"You've done absolutely nothing wrong. You've been a perfectly good wife, just as I was. They just see something younger and prettier, and they go for it.

"You haven't changed at all. It's him who's changed."

"I'm much heavier than I used to be. It's not surprising that he turned to someone much younger..."

And though she kept up a brave front in the office and before her friends and family, the long watches of the night bore witness to her tears of humiliation, and her deep sense of shame and failure.

THE invitation to her godson's wedding came several weeks after Geoffrey's defection, and was addressed to her alone, word having travelled along the grapevine that Geoffrey was no longer on the scene.

The groom was the son of her oldest school friend with whom she had kept in touch over the years and with whom she had many friends in common. They would all be there.

"I don't know if I can face them," she said to Laura.

"Mum," her daughter coaxed patiently on the other end of the phone, "you're your own woman, whatever Dad's done. Go out there and show them that you're a free spirit."

Frances smiled. "I like the sound of that. I just wish I felt more like it."

Margaret's advice was the same, only different.

"Buy something new to wear. And a hat. And if Geoffrey's paying, make it expensive. Make sure they all see what a fool he was to leave you."

★★★★

It wasn't as bad as it might have been. For a start, she was invited to make the journey to the church with a couple she had known for years, so that she wouldn't arrive on her own.

During the champagne and things on sticks, people milled around her, and it became more difficult to maintain her poise.

"So sorry to hear about Geoffrey. To leave you, after all these years!"

"The man's a fool. You're better off without him."

"My dear, how are you coping?"

The men were just as bad. "Any time you need a man around the house, just say the word. I'm a whiz with anything electrical."

She smiled, and turned away to look out of the hotel window at the garden beyond. The trees were beginning to bud and the grass was dotted with purple crocuses. Everything was prettily dappled by a sun which came and went behind the clouds.

But it could have been raining, for all she saw. She tightened her lips against the threatening tears and breathed deeply.

That was the moment when things began to change. She was rescued from her pain by an unlooked-for spurt of anger. How dare he!

How dare Geoffrey subject her to this!

She had been turned into a cliché, an abandoned wife, by a husband who had run off with his secretary. Could anything be more trite, more hackneyed, more embarrassing? She would never forgive him. If he came back tomorrow, she'd let him know there was no chance for reconciliation.

IT was ten months later that Frances met Geoffrey at the vegetable counter in the supermarket.

Frances was examining the avocados and Geoffrey was testing the onions for firmness.

"Frances?"

She swung round. "Oh, it's you."

"You're looking — very well. I almost didn't recognise you."

She knew she was looking good, but didn't react to the compliment. "How are you?"

"Fine, thanks. It's my turn to make dinner, as you can tell."

He sounded reasonably happy, even smug, though Frances thought she could detect uncertainty beneath the smooth veneer.

"Yes. Mine, too." The shock of seeing him had doubled her heartbeat. All their communications had been by phone or letter, virtually since the moment he had left.

She concentrated on her purchases, and moved on again.

He followed.

"Look, Frances —have you time for coffee? We could have a chat, if you like."

"What about?"

He was quite nonplussed. "Oh, everything. Nothing in particular. How you're getting on. That kind of thing."

"I see." She looked at her watch. "Well, I suppose I could spare twenty minutes."

Geoffrey was a little taken aback, but rallied. "Right. I'll meet you in the coffee shop then."

By the time she had stacked her car boot, he was waiting for her at one of the small tables.

"Coffee OK? A little milk, no sugar? You see, I remember."

"Actually I take it black these days, but it doesn't matter. Now, what was it you wanted to talk about?"

He stared. "You've changed."

"Oh, I don't think so. I'm the same person I always was."

He stirred his coffee. "So how's work?"

"Fine, thank you."

"And Margaret?"

"Margaret? Oh, I've no idea. I don't work there any more."

She looked across at him, noticing the thinning hair, the sharp features, the general air of tiredness. "Are you still with Goddard's?"

"Naturally. Am I likely to move after all these years?"

"No, I don't suppose you are." She heard the pity in her own voice, and surprised both of them. Fancy her, the abandoned wife left on the scrap heap, feeling sorry for her husband.

Should she tell him about her new job with a small company which manufactured jewellery, and the training scheme that sent her to college two days a week?

Should she tell Geoffrey about her new friends, about Celia who designed silver jewellery, or John, who was one of her lecturers and who'd shown a definite interest in her, even if she didn't entirely return it?

John was coming for dinner. Should she mention that? She decided not to bother.

Geoffrey was watching her a little apprehensively.

"I really was sorry about hurting you. You do know that, don't you, Frances?"

She looked at him coolly, hiding the wave of pain she felt searing through her quite involuntarily. After all, it was barely a year since he had left. She could expect to feel pain for a long time yet.

"I believe you," she said flatly. "What I still find difficult to understand is why you were so willing to throw away what we had built up together . . .

"But on the other hand," she said quickly, "I'm not altogether sorry. Maybe it was time to move on, for both of us.

"And now, I'm afraid I must love you and leave you."

She stopped dead, as she realised what she had said.

"I didn't mean that, Geoffrey."

"I know you didn't. It's all right."

"Fine." She stood up. "I'll say goodbye, then."

Without a backward glance, she swung away from the table, out of the dark little coffee shop, and into the sunlight of the late afternoon. ■

Sam's Legacy

by Ann Monks

It wasn't just a tumbledown wall he was restoring — it was a young man's battered confidence . . .

ALAN opened the cottage door and stepped outside. He had to duck his head to avoid hitting it on the low stone lintel. It was like everything in the cottage, he thought sourly — too low and too small for him.

He knew if Jean were here, she'd be urging him on, trying to build his confidence, but Jean was out at work — and he was at home without a job.

They'd moved to Embury a month ago, after both he and Jean had been made redundant. They'd both looked for work but it was Jean who'd found a job first, as a district nurse.

"Where are we going to live, though?" Alan had said.

There was one property in their price range — a tiny cottage five miles out.

And now Alan found himself alone in the cottage every morning after Jean left for her daily round.

"There's plenty to do in the house before you need to go looking for work," Jean had said, when he'd come back from yet another fruitless job search.

Then, when she'd seen the depression in his eyes, she'd added, "Mind you, it's a shame to waste this good weather. Why don't you make a start on the garden? We could grow our own vegetables. That would be a help."

And that was why he was standing here at 8.30 in the morning, looking at an overgrown garden and a tumbledown wall.

"A car came round the bend too fast and ran into it," Tim Welsby, the owner of the nearby farm, had explained when he'd handed over the keys on the first day. "It was the day after old Sam moved out.

"He keeps offering to rebuild it for me but it's far too heavy a job for him at his age and I haven't got the time.

"It's a dry-stone wall, you see, and there's not many I'd trust with it."

He'd patted the warm boulders affectionately.

Now, Alan grimaced at the wall with no affection at all. He'd been a draughtsman. He could manage painting and decorating, but building a dry-stone wall was out of his league.

He sighed. If he made a start, perhaps he could block up most of the holes in it by lunchtime.

By mid afternoon, Alan had managed to complete only a few feet.

"You'll not be leaving it like that, will you?"

He looked up into a pair of faded blue eyes set in a face tanned and wrinkled by many years of working outdoors.

"And what's wrong with it?" he asked, instantly on his guard.

"Well —" the old man drew on his pipe "— I'm not saying it's that bad — for city folk, like.

"But it'll never stay up. It's none too safe."

He gave the wall a prod with his walking stick, and as if to illustrate the point, the last stone Alan had placed there wobbled precariously.

Alan made himself count to ten. This was just what he needed — a know-it-all coming along and pulling his best efforts to pieces.

"It'll be all right," he said.

"No, no. It won't do at all. What do you think will happen if one of Tim's cows bashes into it when he brings them down for milking?"

The old man shook his head. "No, no. It'll have to come down. Don't worry, lad. I'll give you a hand."

Alan stared in disbelief as the old man sat himself down on the one good part of the wall. From there, he gave directions, pointing with his stick to the stones Alan should use, and tapping his cane impatiently whenever Alan picked up the wrong ones.

Alan didn't try to argue. If it doesn't look right, I can always take it down and start again tomorrow when he's not here, he thought.

But slowly, as the wall grew higher, it did look right — looked right and felt right — and he began to develop a sneaking admiration for the old man and his expert knowledge.

"The mistake most folk make," the old man said as he directed the building operation, "is that they think it's one wall and they try to build it like that and then it falls down because it's not strong enough."

Alan straightened up, stretched his aching back and groaned. It looked like he was in for some heavy work for quite a while yet.

The old man grinned and Alan knew he'd read his thoughts.

"It's not one wall, you see," he repeated. "It looks like it, but it's not. It's two walls, running side by side and linked. After all, two's stronger than one, isn't it?" He patted the completed section of wall to emphasise his point.

Alan stooped to pick up some small stones.

"And what do you think you're doing with them?" the old man asked.

"Surely they're much too small to be of any use?" Alan replied.

"Too small!"

For a moment Alan thought his mentor was going to explode.

"They're your most important pieces after your foundation stones, they are. They're your 'heartings'."

He reached down and picked one of them up.

"See," he said, this is what goes in the centre of your wall.

"Even walls have to have hearts, you know."

IT took three hours of long, hard labour before the short stretch of wall that fronted the road had risen as many feet.

The summer sun was out and Alan was starting to feel hot and very tired after his exertions.

The interior of the cottage had never looked more cool or inviting, but the old man wouldn't let him break off for the cup of coffee he offered him.

34

"You've got a full head of steam up now, lad. It'd be a shame to stop. Anyway, you'd like as not stiffen up, seeing as you're not used to this kind of work."

He reached into his coat pocket as he spoke and produced two apples.

"Here, chew on this."

Alan accepted the apple docilely, at a loss for words.

Unused to this kind of work indeed, he thought, wincing as he bent to pick up another stone. It wasn't just this kind of work he wasn't used to, it was this kind of life, and — he looked balefully at the old man — these kind of people!

"Right, that's not bad for a start. We've done a good day's work there." And before Alan could pick him up on the 'We', the old man eased himself up as a bus came into sight and waved his cane in the air for it to stop.

Alan had to smile to himself. This wasn't a scheduled stop, but he didn't like to think of the consequences for the bus driver if he kept going.

"Well, thank you." Alan was surprised to hear himself say that. He hadn't exactly welcomed the old man's interference but he had to acknowledge it had made a difference.

The three foot section of wall, which it had taken all afternoon to build, was sound and steady and Tim Welsby's cows would be safe when they came past for milking.

As it happened, he'd finished only just in time, for no sooner had the bus disappeared with the old man on board than the herd flooded down the lane.

Tim stopped by the gate.

"I see you've met old Sam," he said, smiling.

"So that's who it was."

"He's a bit of a character, is our Sam."

ALAN had never thought that he would feel affectionate towards a heap of stones, but he did and that night he told Jean about Sam and how the old man had helped him.

"I'm not surprised he wanted to see the wall done right after all the years he lived here," Alan said. "But he never even let on who he was."

"Probably in a small community like this he's used to everyone knowing," Jean said. "This isn't the big city now."

"No, you're right," Alan said, and was surprised to find that for the first time since they'd come here, he didn't hanker after their former home.

The next morning, Alan was up early and out even before Jean. It promised to be another hot day, and he was looking forward to making further progress with his wall.

He bent to sort the stones he would need as a bus pulled up.

He heard the door hiss open and the bus pull away.

He looked up to find himself gazing straight into Sam's wrinkled face. He noticed the stones in Alan's hands.

"And what do you think you're doing with those?"Sam said.

"They're heartings," Alan said.

"Ay, I can see that, but it's not heartings you're needing now, 'through stones'. We've got to link these two walls together. Tie 'em in — give 'em some strength. Now then —" Sam looked about him keenly "— there's some likely ones."

He pointed imperiously with his stick to a pile of long, knobbly stones that lay a few feet away. With an inward sigh, Alan dropped the heartings and went to fetch the ones Sam had indicated.

There was obviously no way round it. Sam had adopted him as apprentice dry-stone waller and he might as well just accept it.

OVER the next few weeks, under Sam's eagle eye, Alan rebuilt the wall around the garden. He even pulled down and rebuilt from scratch parts that he could have just repaired, so that the whole wall was a single, strong construction.

He'd been both longing for and dreading the day the last stone was put in place. It was the end of a useful task, but he knew that now he would once again have to start what he was sure would only be a fruitless search for work.

"Well, what do you think?" he asked Sam.

The old man nodded slowly.

"It's not bad for a beginner — and you'll get better with a bit of practice."

Coming from Sam this was high praise indeed and Alan felt a glow of affection for the old man. One thing was wrong with Sam's grand ideas, though, and Alan told him.

"There's not much chance of more practice, is there?" he said. "I've no more wall to do here."

"Not here you haven't, but I was talking to Tim the other day and he wouldn't mind his wall in the northern pasture redoing. That should give you more than enough practice."

Sam grinned at him. "Mind you, I wouldn't be able to get up there as often as I have here. You'd have to get on with that on your own . . ."

He let the suggestion hang doubtfully in the air, and Alan had to hide the smile that came to his lips.

He'd got to know Sam pretty well over the last few weeks and he knew when he was being baited.

"Maybe I should take a look at it before I commit myself," he suggested.

"Ay, happen you should," Sam replied.

ALL through the rest of the summer and the autumn, Alan was kept busy. Tim had what seemed like miles of damaged wall that needed rebuilding.

On good days, Sam would walk over the fields to sit and offer advice and the two of them built up quite a friendship, but as autumn gave way to winter, Alan saw less and less of him.

Sometimes Jean, coming home for lunch, would see him waiting for the bus in his usual place, sitting on the wall of their garden, always munching on an apple or pulling on his pipe, but generally Sam seemed to keep himself pretty much to himself.

One evening, Alan came home late and found the cottage in darkness when he would have expected to find Jean there.

She came in an hour later, tired and pale.

"I've got some bad news," she said, and suddenly Alan remembered the night he'd come home and said the same words before he told her he'd lost his job.

He suddenly felt frightened that this new world he was building was under threat. His chest tightened as he waited for her next words.

"It's Sam," she said. "He's dead."

Just four words, but they stirred up a powerful mixture of emotions: grief for the old man who had become a loved and trusted friend, anger at his loss — and guilt . . .

How much of a friend had he been to Sam, he chided himself, when he hadn't even visited him to see how he was getting on?

"He hasn't been too good over the last few weeks. I've popped in a couple of times to see him." Jean's words broke into his thoughts.

"You never said."

"He didn't want me to. He said you weren't to come visiting him when you had so much work on and he'd be up and about in the spring to supervise you again."

"If I'd known, I could have —"

"I'm sorry, love, but you know what Sam was like." Jean reached out to touch her husband's hand. "It was what he wanted."

Alan didn't say anything. It was, indeed, what Sam would have wanted, he thought. A peaceful ending. He never could stand fuss and bother.

The next day, Alan went back up to carry on working on Tim's walls, but all the pleasure had gone out of the job.

Winter was here with a vengeance now, and the skies that only a few weeks ago had been a cheerful blue were now the same colour as the rough, grey stones.

There seemed little to distinguish sky from earth. It was all so drab and dreary, and Alan shivered inside his thick coat.

The stones, unwarmed by sun, were clammy and awkward in Alan's hands, and where only the day before he had seemed able to find exactly the right stone for the right place, now none would fit.

He went home far from pleased with his day's work.

The following day, the snow blew in.

For two weeks, Alan stayed indoors, and to take his mind off Sam, set about the redecoration of the cottage which, with all the dry-stone wall work, had been neglected.

When the snow finally melted, he bumped into Tim in the lane.

"How're you getting on with the northern pasture?"

"I was thinking of leaving it until the spring," Alan said.

Tim nodded. "That's all right by me. But I'd like to get it finished before June. I'll be wanting to use it for the cows when they calve."

Alan didn't respond. Spring was a long way off, but deep inside he knew he was going to find it difficult to go back to build the wall. Since Sam's death, he seemed to have lost all interest in it.

IT was February before Alan thought of looking outside the cottage for work that needed doing. Throughout the winter, he'd gone into Embury each day to see if there were any new jobs advertised, but there was nothing, and he was glad to have the excuse of the cottage needing decorating. It kept him busy.

It was Jean who suggested he start working outside again.

"The grass verge between the wall and the road could do with clearing. After you finished the wall last year, you and Sam were so keen to get started on Tim's walls, you didn't have time to get round to it."

Alan nodded. He still winced inside at the mention of Sam's name, but he hid it from Jean. It reminded him of a time when he had started to hope again. She was right, though, the grass verge did need clearing.

The next day was Saturday. It was the first fine day of the year and Alan filled the wheelbarrow with the stones that had been left lying there since the previous summer. He worked his way along the wall.

"Looks like it could do with cutting as well, and there's a briar there that'll need to come out." Jean had donned her coat and gardening gloves and come to help.

"Alan," she said, "look at this."

He squatted down beside her. Almost in the middle of the verge, in fact, so much so that it looked as though it had been deliberately planted there, was a slender wisp of a plant, tiny leaves attempting to unfurl at its tip.

"I'll get that out easily enough," Alan said.

"No." Jean stayed his hand. "Look." Gently she spread one of the miniature leaves.

"Do you know what it is?"

"Just a seed sown by the wind or dropped by a bird?"

"No," Jean said. "Sam sowed this."

"What do you mean?"

"Don't you remember?" Jean said. "This is where Sam used to sit and wait for the bus."

"And tell me how to build the wall," Alan said to himself.

"He was always eating an apple. He even used to eat the core, but he'd drop the seeds right here. That's what this is — it's Sam's apple tree."

They stood and looked at it in silence.

"Pity it won't get much bigger," Jean said. "When Tim puts the cows out in the far pasture again and brings them up and down the lane, it's going to get trampled on.

"We could try moving it."

"No!" Alan was surprised at the strength in his voice.

"It mightn't survive, and anyway, this is where Sam planted it. This is where it should stay. We won't move it. We'll protect it. I'll build it a wall. Just a little one to start off with, but it can get bigger each year. I can use these."

He picked up the stones in the wheelbarrow, the heartings that had been left over from last year.

They were rough on his hands, hands made soft by a winter indoors, but the warmth of the stone ran up through his fingers and into his body, pushing out the cold depression that had engulfed him.

For the first time in months he felt good again.

Jean smiled at him and he smiled back. Sam had been right, two were always stronger than one, whether it was walls or people.

It had taken Jean to bring him to a new life here and Sam to teach him an old skill. If he gave up now, the walls would crumble. It was his commitment and determination that were the through stones, holding it all together.

"I'd better get a move on then, hadn't I? I daresay Tim will be wanting me to start up again on the north pasture soon."

"Great!" Jean's face lit up. "I'll come and give you a hand after I've made us a coffee."

"Coffee?" Alan looked at her and laughed. "An apple will do me just fine!" ■

On The Eve Of The Wedding

by Shirley Worrall

It was only natural she would have doubts — but not, surely, about her fiancé's feelings?

LISA knew that if she didn't escape within the next ten seconds she would go totally and utterly insane. Carefully she put down her untouched glass of sherry, cut Aunt Clara off in mid-sentence and announced, "I'm going for a walk."

A sea of horrified faces stared at her.

"You can't!" her mother gasped. "You might bump into Joe. It's unlucky to see the groom on the eve of the wedding."

"I'll walk towards the village. Joe will be busy checking the animals, so I'll be quite safe!"

She grabbed her jacket on the way out, stepped into the fresh air and walked smartly down the road leading into the village.

What a mess! she thought.

Her parents' house was filled with relations, eagerly awaiting the following day's spectacle. Joe's home was filled with guests, more of his many relations.

The cars would be arriving in the morning, suitably swathed in white ribbons. The photographer would be loading his camera. The florist —

Lisa ran a trembling hand across her face. She could cope with drivers, photographers and florists. She could even cope with dozens of shocked, bewildered guests.

It was the rest of her life that she couldn't cope with . . .

She had to tell Joe that she couldn't marry him. But even that wouldn't be too difficult, as Lisa suspected he was trying to find a way of telling her the same thing.

Lisa had known early that morning when Aunt Clara, Joe's great-aunt, had produced old photographs of Joe's first wedding, that she couldn't go through with it.

Aunt Clara hadn't realised that showing old wedding photographs on the eve of another wedding was tactless. She had merely been proving to Aunt Joan that she hadn't worn green at Joe's first wedding.

Somehow Lisa kept smiling but all that registered was the look on Joe's face as he'd stared at the photographs.

Lisa hadn't been able to miss the stunned expression on his face. It was as if he'd forgotten just how much he had loved Sylvie, and as if he was shocked to find himself marrying again.

The look on his face as he turned to Lisa chilled her. For a moment she thought he was going to call the whole thing off. But no.

"Time I was going," he said awkwardly.

He kissed Lisa briefly, the kiss of a stranger. "See you at the church."

And then he'd gone, to do all those "things" he said he had to do. Or, as Lisa suspected, to lose himself in memories of Sylvie . . .

AT fifteen, Lisa had thought of Joe as nothing more than the dull, if handsome, farmer who had married the most gorgeous–looking girl Lisa had ever known.

Lisa took no notice of Joe but imitated everything Sylvie did. Sylvie was French, and, although she'd lived in England for several years, she had that innate French chic.

Lisa had spent hours in front of her mirror copying how she looked and what she wore.

Then, when Sylvie had died, only six months after her wedding, the whole village went into shock.

Lisa's mother immediately took on the rôle of mothering Joe.

One day she'd asked Lisa to run the five hundred yards to the farmhouse to give Joe her latest offering — steak and kidney pudding.

"Do I have to?" Lisa had groaned, uncomfortable around Joe these days. "Yes!"

Lisa had gone to the farm, knocked on the door, and, receiving no reply, had walked round to the back and opened the kitchen door.

Joe was sitting at the table with his back to her. His head was in his hands . . . and he was crying.

Intruding on his private pain like that stunned and embarrassed her so much she couldn't move, couldn't even clear her throat to announce her presence.

Joe turned, as if sensing her presence. Horrified, he brushed his hands across his face. "Lisa —"

"Mum asked me to leave this," she said quickly.

"Lisa, it's all right." His voice was gentle, as if he were trying to coax a wild animal. "Don't be frightened."

Lisa remembered dropping the basket on the table and running wildly from Joe's farm.

Instead of heading home, she'd run up the hill and hadn't stopped until she reached the top. Then, she'd thrown herself down on the ground and lain there breathing heavily.

Joe had been wrong, she hadn't been frightened — just incredibly moved. She had just finished reading Wuthering Heights and there, down at the farmhouse, she'd come upon a living, breathing Heathcliff.

For days, Lisa's every thought had been of Joe. Her dreams were full of him too, a confusing mixture of Joe and Heathcliff.

Her future was suddenly clear, she was going to marry Joe Carpenter.

AT 18, Lisa began a catering course at the nearby college. It was all she could think of training for that didn't involve moving away from home, and therefore away from Joe.

"You'll meet new friends," her mother decided with satisfaction.

"I don't want new friends," Lisa had said.

"Lisa," her mother had said gently. "I understand how you feel about Joe but, believe me, you'll get over him . . ."

A look of hurt crossed Lisa's face.

"You have no idea how I feel, Mum, do you?"

"He's too old for you, love," her mother pointed out.

"What's ten years?" Lisa scoffed.

"He's done more living than you," her mother had persisted. "He's been married, lost his wife . . ."

Lisa had grown up enough to realise that Joe wasn't ready to love, but she'd also grown up enough to realise that there would never be anyone else in her life.

She no longer confused him with the fictional Heathcliff, and she was prepared to wait — in the hope that, one day, he would see her as more than the kid from up the road.

Her catering course was Heaven-sent.

"Joe, would you let me cook you lunch on Sunday? I need all the practice I can get."

"My dear girl, you can cook me lunch any Sunday you like!"

"Joe, Mum's busy in her kitchen. Can I come and borrow yours so that I can do some breadmaking?"

"It's all yours. So long as I get to taste it!"

This is it, Lisa had thought. Didn't they say that the way to a man's heart was via his stomach?

They'd shared countless meals together, with Lisa asking his opinion on every mouthful. She couldn't really have cared less what he thought of her cooking, she was just happy to be with him.

"It's time I repaid the compliment," Joe had said one day with a grin. "Don't panic, I'm not offering to cook! I thought we could go out for a meal one evening."

Lisa had hoped and longed for this moment.

Making sure he couldn't change his mind, Lisa had replied, "When?"

"Whenever suits you."

"Tomorrow?"

Joe had laughed at her eagerness. "Tomorrow," he'd agreed.

Lisa had spent the next day going through her wardrobe for something to wear for what was, she decided, the most important day of her life.

Judging by the admiration in Joe's eyes, the havoc she had caused in her bedroom had been well worth it.

It should have been a perfect evening. Should have been.

Midway through the first course, Joe had said, "About that day you walked into the kitchen —"

"It was a long time ago," Lisa had murmured.

"I wish you hadn't witnessed that," Joe had said, "but you're right, Lisa, it was a long time ago. I'm over all that. What I'm trying to say is that I don't want you feeling sorry for me."

"Sorry for you?" Lisa had echoed, stunned.

"Isn't that what this is all about?" he'd asked softly. "Don't think I don't enjoy having you around, Lisa, but it's not necessary."

"It was never sympathy," Lisa had said, hurt by his words. "I happen to enjoy your company."

He hadn't commented until they were midway through their main course and then he had put the seal on the evening by saying carefully, "You're very sweet, Lisa, but you ought to be with people your own age."

Lisa had wanted to throw her wine over him.

Sweet! She had loved him for years. Everything she had ever done, she had done because she loved him. And he thought she was sweet. Not beautiful, clever, witty, or devastating — sweet!

When Joe had stopped the car outside her house, instead of thanking him for a lovely evening, she'd said furiously, "I'm twenty, Joe — old enough to choose my own friends. Now if you don't want me hanging around, just say so. Don't use the difference in our ages as an excuse."

"Don't be silly," he'd said. "I just think you need some time with people your own age."

"Fine!" Lisa had cried, jumping out of the car. "You rot on your farm, Joe Carpenter, and I'll spend time with people my own age!"

FOR the next few days, she'd alternated between tears of humiliation, a raging fury and a sense of loss that threatened to overwhelm her.

She hadn't gone near Joe — pride kept her away.

She made sure she was out almost every night.

A month or so later, she'd bumped into Joe in the village.

"I haven't seen you around, Lisa," he'd said curiously. "I've missed you. What have you been up to?"

"I'm fine," she'd told him airily, "I've been busy having fun with people my own age."

"That's good. I'm glad."

The only consolation in that infuriating statement was that he hadn't looked particularly glad.

She began working in a large, modern hotel in town so that their paths crossed even less frequently.

Two weeks before her 21st birthday, Lisa had met Joe in town and invited him to the party she was having.

"Although most of the guests will be my age," she'd warned him.

"I'm not a crumbling antique," Joe had snapped. "Ten years is nothing!"

Touché, Lisa had thought drily.

Lisa had great plans for being the life and soul of her party, giving the impression that she was having far too much fun to notice Joe.

Then, early on the morning of her birthday, the roses had arrived. Two dozen perfect red roses.

The card said simply: Happy Birthday, Lisa. Joe.

There was no special significance to red roses, she'd told herself sharply, but she couldn't help touching the velvet petals.

Joe had arrived at her party looking more attractive than ever. Just like Heathcliff, Lisa had thought.

He'd handed her a carefully wrapped parcel and without opening it, Lisa knew it was a paperweight to add to her collection.

She'd opened it carefully and then gasped. "Oh, Joe, it's beautiful. It's Victorian, isn't it?"

Smiling, Joe had nodded.

"I'll always treasure it," she'd promised softly.

Then, the proud Lisa who had vowed to ignore Joe, found huge tears forming pools in her eyes.

Joe had lifted her chin, his gaze questioning.

"I've missed you," Lisa had admitted softly.

"I've missed you, too." Then, as if he couldn't quite believe how such a ludicrous thing had happened, he'd taken her hands in his and said, "I love you, Lisa . . ."

Eighteen months later, Joe had asked her to marry him and now — she had to tell him that she couldn't go through with it.

Lisa walked into the village and up the hill, making a three mile trek of the five hundred yards to the farm.

Taking a deep, shaky breath, she walked round to the back of the house and stepped inside the kitchen. She half expected to see him sitting at the table, as he had been all those years ago when he'd been grieving for Sylvie. But the kitchen was empty.

Just about to call out, she was suddenly startled by the sound of Joe's deep laughter.

She opened the sitting-room door and saw him laughing at Peg, his faithful collie, who was having a great time sending the contents of a box of confetti flying everywhere.

Joe's laughter died as he turned and saw Lisa. "I bet Aunt Clara doesn't know you're here," he said quietly.

Lisa tried to smile but failed. "No."

Joe regarded her steadily. "I expect it's unlucky to throw confetti before the event, too."

Unable to speak, Lisa nodded and two stray tears rolled down her face.

"I can't do it, Joe," Lisa whispered. "And I don't think you can, either."

"What do you mean?"

"I can't marry you. I knew I couldn't go through with it this morning," Lisa burst out. "When I saw you looking at that photo of you and Sylvie on your wedding day, I knew I couldn't go through life being second best and trying to live up to —"

"Hey," Joe cut her off. "You're not second best, Lisa. You should know that. I couldn't love you any more than I do."

Joe stared at her. "If I looked — What was it? Shocked? Then it was only because it seemed so long ago. It was like looking at a perfect stranger. Two perfect strangers."

He looked into her doubtful face and said quietly, "You're right, it was more than that. It was remembering the doubts. I was in love with Sylvie and she loved me, but even on our wedding day, I couldn't help thinking it was going to need more than that.

"Looking at that photo this morning, I knew that the marriage wouldn't have worked. We were in love, yes, but it was a young love, an immature love — a love built on little more than dreams."

Lisa felt the warmth of his love for her. She understood and she loved Joe for being so honest — with her and with himself.

"And," Joe went on, "I have no doubts about this marriage. Even when my lunatic of a future wife turns up with her nonsensical ideas!"

Lisa slipped her arms around him, rested her head on his shoulder, and wondered if anyone could be happier.

"Tomorrow, my love," Joe said firmly, "you'll be in that church vowing to love, honour and obey me."

"Cherish," Lisa murmured. "Love, honour and cherish," she explained smiling.

"There's no obey?"

Lisa laughed. "Sorry."

"You mean I have to endow you with all my worldly goods and all I get in return is cherished?"

"'Fraid so."

Joe pulled a face. "Not much of a deal, is it?"

Then laughing, into her outraged face, Joe lifted her off the ground and kissed her . . .

The Great Holiday Adventure

by Rita Williamson

It wasn't what any of them had expected and, surprisingly, that's what made it so memorable . . .

I T was the bestest holiday ever! Matthew Walters, just seven years old, was quite certain about that. He couldn't wait to go back to school after the Easter holidays and tell Jimmy Rogers about it. He'd be green, absolutely green, with envy!

Oh, it had been brill!

It was funny really, because Matthew hadn't wanted to go when Mummy had said that they were going to Wales.

Matty knew you didn't have to go in a plane or even on a boat to get to Wales. You just went in the car.

Just the rotten, rotten car for hours and hours, with Sally kicking him all the way and baby Scott falling asleep and dribbling on him. Even Luke the dog had been given a pill and lay in the back of the car fast asleep.

Matty couldn't even play games with Mummy because she had to do the driving. Daddy should have been driving, but he was too busy at work to come on holiday until next week.

Just when Mummy stopped the car and said, "Here we are," it started to rain and the clouds made it so dark that it felt like winter.

Sally and Matty had scrambled out of the car, glad not to be cooped up any longer. But Matty was angry with Mummy for bringing them here and he was angry with Daddy for staying at home.

He was angry at the whole world for making them go to Wales.

He slammed the car door hard and looked fiercely at the cottage.

"Is this it? Cor, what a dump!"

"Matthew!" Mummy's voice sounded sore, like she was trying not to cry.

Matty bit back the other nasty words he had been going to come out with and scuffed the toe of his shoe on the path instead.

Mummy's eyes looked sad, but she smiled bravely at them and said in a jolly voice, "This is our holiday cottage, children. It's called Talyllyn. Isn't that nice?"

Matthew's lip trembled with the unfairness of it all. Just because Daddy's business wasn't doing so well, they had to have a holiday in a scruffy old garden shed!

When the door had swung open, though, Matthew Walters realised just how wrong he'd been . . .

To his amazement, the place was really magic!

When Mummy opened the door, you were right inside the lounge. Off the step and on to the sofa, just like that!

It was all dark and shadowy, just like a cave, and the ceiling was dead low!

Matthew was amazed. The walls were brick, and left so that you could see them. There was no wallpaper or anything, they were just painted white and looked sort of nice.

And then, when Mummy turned on the lamps, all these metal things (Mummy said they were horse brasses) shone like gold. It looked like a cave full of buried treasure.

THEY inspected every corner. Luke the dog did the difficult bits under the sofa and behind the curtains.

Just by the front door was a bedroom and it was the prettiest room Matty had ever seen. Even Sally's Barbie didn't have a room like that!

There were flowers on the walls, flowers on the curtains and flowers on the bed covers. Everything was frilly and flouncy.

It was Mummy's room. It was just like her, all soft and pretty and smelling of summer.

Mummy found the kitchen and pulled open cupboard doors and looked inside drawers.

The kitchen had a window over the sink, but it didn't look over the garden; it looked out on to some steps that went upwards. Straight up, really high — to the garden.

Matty's amazement grew. Their garden was up a mountain! What an upside-down sort of place Wales was.

"Where are we going to sleep, Mummy?" Sally asked.

"In the attic room."

Cor! Those stairs were steep. It was like being on a ship, running up and down the rigging. No — Matty corrected himself — it was like climbing a mountain!

He could see two weeks of bliss stretching ahead of him. Every morning when he got up, and every night when he went to bed, he could play mountain-climbers.

At the top of the twisty, turny stairs was a whole room with two little beds and a cot in it. There was no door, nothing, just this whole room at the top of the stairs. It was brill — and the fun didn't stop there!

Every morning, just like magic, the sink was full of woodlice and Matty would chase them round and round the stainless steel circus, till Mummy made him stop.

Mummy didn't like woodlice — not one little bit — and by the third day she gave him a badge she'd made that said, Chief Woodlice Catcher.

It was his job to clean out the sink before Mummy got there. He felt really grown up, just like Daddy.

Matty's face clouded momentarily. He wished Daddy was here.

ONE day, when it was sunny, Mummy took them for a drive. They went to see a castle — a real castle. It was so old it was falling down, but it had towers and dungeons and battlements.

Matthew and Sally played knights and dragons. The man in the shop that sold postcards said there were still dragons in Wales . . .

They went down a mine, too. A real one where men used to work in the olden days. Sally cried because of the dark, but Matty thought it was great. They made real coal as well — just dug it out of the ground; didn't have to go to the shop or anything.

That was another good thing about their holiday cottage. It had a fire. A real fire.

You had to put coal on with little brass tongs that hung by the side of the grate.

It was best at night, Matty decided. Mummy would sit on the sofa, while Scotty would fall asleep at one end under Mummy's jacket and Matthew and Sally lay on the rug in front of the fire and just stared into the orange flames.

Mummy smiled a lot and made up a story for them all.

Of course, the holiday got really brill when Daddy came. They'd been there a whole week by the time he got there at tea-time on Saturday.

Mummy was pleased to see him and so was Luke, who bounded all over him and left paw-prints on his trousers. Matty wanted to show his father everything about their holiday cottage, but instead, he was put to bed early with Sally and Scott.

It was cosy up in the little room over the lounge as Matty lay listening to his parents talking downstairs.

"Oh, Jim, I'm so glad you're here. It's been horrible!"

"Hey —" his father's voice was soothing "— what's wrong?"

"It's dreadful, that's what's wrong. There's no TV, no central heating. The temperature in the bathroom hovers just above freezing all the time and it rains woodlice in the kitchen!"

"Come on, honey, it can't be that bad."

"It is!" Mummy cried and Matthew heard Daddy saying, "there, there" and, "it'll be all right".

Then Mummy stopped crying and started being angry.

"Oh, will it? That's because you're here, is it? The great boss-man come to take charge? This was meant to be our holiday, Jim — a chance for us to really be together as a family — and you spend half of it at the office!"

"Look, love, you know I had to —"

"No you didn't! Someone else could have done it. It could have waited two miserable weeks. But we can't wait. The kids can't wait to grow up until you're ready to watch!

"Did you know Scotty's nearly walking now? He'll be riding a bike before you get to spend any time with him!"

Upstairs, in his rooftop hideaway, Matty trembled.

There was silence downstairs for a long time and all he could hear were little sniffs from his mother and soft murmurs from his father.

"Jenny, love, I had to stay and finish the job. Look, if I don't work all the hours I can, there will be no money for holidays like this . . ."

"Holiday? Holiday? Do you think it's a holiday looking after three kids in the back of beyond, all by myself?"

Mummy's voice was scratchy and Matthew didn't like it, so he pulled the soft blankets up over his ears until he couldn't hear any more.

IT was still dark when Matty woke up. He didn't know what had wakened him. Maybe it was Sally whimpering, because she always carried on when there was a storm, and there was a storm now — a really good one!

The wind howled and screeched around the roof. It sounded, to Matthew, like a monster. It must be one of those dragons that the man in the castle told him about, getting ready to rip the roof right off.

"Come on, you can come into my bed," Matthew offered bravely, and he and Sally scrambled under the bedclothes and had a tug of war with the covers.

Exhausted, they lay giggling for a minute, saying "shush" and "quiet" in case they woke Scotty, when . . . Splosh! A big drop of cold water landed right in Matty's face.

And another, and another, until a steady stream of water was splashing on to his pillow.

He and Sally stared at each other in the dim light and began to giggle again. What was going on?

Just at that moment, Mummy came upstairs to find out. Matty told her about the rain and she winced as though she'd felt a sudden pain. She sometimes did that when Daddy rang to say he'd be late home.

She felt the beds and the carpet and then snatched Scotty up out of his cot and told them to follow her. As they were going down the stairs, Matty thought that Mummy's face was wet, too. Maybe it was the rain.

Daddy was fast asleep in the big flowery bed and stayed fast asleep even when Matthew climbed over to get in beside him.

What fun, Matthew thought . . . Mummy, Daddy, Sally, Scott and him all in one bed.

IN the darkness, lying rigid with tension, Jenny Walters could feel the soft warmth of her children crowding against her body. It felt good and she realised how long it had been since they had all snuggled up like this.

Slowly she let her body relax.

She looked across at Jim, asleep in the moonlight, and smiled. Was he in for a shock when he woke up! She stifled a giggle and felt the traumas of the night begin to fade.

Weren't kids funny? She'd worried herself sick about bringing them to a rickety cottage with nothing to do except watch the scenery, but they'd taken to it like ducks to water.

She thought back over all they'd done: playing games, making toast, watching the fire, walking the dog. They'd had a whale of a time.

Did the kids worry because there was no video? No, they chased woodlice round the kitchen sink!

Did they worry that there was no water chute? No, they went to the cupboard and picked out a jig-saw.

Did they worry that there was no central heating? No, it meant they had hot-water bottles!

They hadn't seen discomfort, only adventure, and, where she had sulked, they had revelled in the change of routine.

So what if the business had gone through a bad patch and their bank account had been cut in half, she thought suddenly. They still had each other and there were still good things in life that didn't rely on money.

A long-forgotten, careworn corner of her heart that used to delight in adventures suddenly swelled with happiness. She'd forgotten how to have fun. Well, not any longer!

★★★★

Jim Walters woke to chaos. Worse, chaos at close quarters. His wife, three children and a large dog were going wild in his bed.

He found himself pinned to the bed by a ladle, which was obviously meant to be a pirate's cutlass. At the other end of the ladle, his wife twinkled a merry smile at him.

"Well, lookee here, me hearties, our prisoner is awake!" A chorus of rather smaller pirates "Yo, ho ho'd" in response.

"What on earth's going on?" Jim Walters muttered weakly.

"This is the good ship Lollipop," Matty told him, "and you are our prisoner. If you don't do what we say, we'll feed you to the woodlice!"

Jim Walters wasn't too concerned by these threats. He wasn't really paying attention. He was staring at his wife.

He didn't know what had happened, but Jenny was smiling at him again. It had been such a long time since she'd laughed and smiled at him, he'd almost forgotten how lovely she was.

Seconds later, pinned to the mattress with two children on his chest and a dog across his knees, he found himself agreeing to their terms.

He was going to walk the dog, play on the swings, go and buy bread, come home to play a tune on the rickety old piano and listen to Mummy read from one of the books they'd found up on the high shelf.

A little while later, propped up against the old brass bedstead, sipping at a cup of tea, Jim listened to his wife tell of the night's traumas. Perched cross-legged at the end of the bed, her long dark hair in a pony-tail, she looked like the young girl he'd married.

"I'm sorry about last night Jim," she said. "I never meant to argue with you as soon as you got here."

"I'm the one who should be apologising," he said. "Fancy leaving you here on your own with the kids. You were right; I don't see them enough, and I should have tried harder to get away last week."

He planted a tentative kiss on her forehead. "Can you bear to stay here till the end of the week, or do you want me to take you home?"

Jenny Walters sat up in shock. "Go home? Don't be silly! Don't you realise we're in the middle of an adventure here? There are woodlice to catch, crumpets to toast! We can't go home now!"

"You sound like Matty."

"Good!" Jenny Walters smiled at her husband. "Matty taught me a lesson last night. Life is what you make it. He didn't mind that his bed was soaked. To him, it was all part of Life's Great Adventure. To me, it was a disaster. I suddenly realised I'd become a miserable old scaredy-cat."

She smiled at her husband. "It's the same with the business. You're having a bit of a tough time, and I've been acting like it's the end of the world. I've been too busy worrying to make the best of the good things we've got."

They exchanged a kiss that was full of apologies and promises, and Jenny pulled away reluctantly.

"Come on, Jim, you'd better get up or Captain Matty will be here with a fistful of woodlice."

The words were no sooner out of her mouth than her son scampered into the tiny, frilly room.

"Mum! Dad!" Two little people, bursting with news, leapt on to the bed followed by an excited dog. Scotty, on all fours, brought up the rear, gurgling contentedly.

Breathless, happiness bursting from every pore, their son and daughter announced their news.

"Oh, Mum, this is the bestest holiday ever! There are sheeps in the garden!" ■

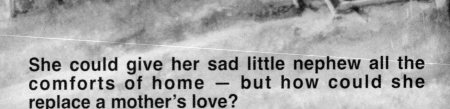

Distant Heart

by Teresa Ashby

She could give her sad little nephew all the comforts of home — but how could she replace a mother's love?

S O this was Jeannie's boy. He stood on the platform like a little grey rag doll as the two-carriage train snaked off down the line into the distance.

Everything about him indicated sadness.

He was dressed entirely in grey except for his scuffed brown shoes and even his pinched little face had a greyish tinge.

She bit her lip to stop herself from crying. He needed her to be strong for him.

Jill took a step or two towards him and he seemed to back away

slightly, his big round brown eyes watching her suspiciously.

"Jamie?" she said, softly. "Jamie, is it you?" He was the image of Jeannie, but she couldn't dwell on that now.

Never taking his eyes off her for a moment, he nodded and bent down to pick up the big holdall at his side.

"I'm your Auntie Jill," Jill said cheerfully, coming forward now and reaching for his bag.

She tried to relieve him of it, but his grip on the handles tightened. Taking a deep breath, she forced a smile. "OK, Jamie, you carry it."

Her heart was pounding and she felt ridiculously nervous.

Silly to be frightened of an eight-year-old boy! Absolutely ridiculous!

Jamie had stopped at the station entrance and was staring at her — and looking more like his mother, Jeannie, than he had any right to.

All the strength seemed to leave her . . .

★★★★

Jillian and Jean. Twins. Their mother had dressed them identically, but it had soon become clear that they were as different as could be.

Jeannie was the soppy one. She fell in and out of love as often as Jill washed her hair. It was inevitable she would marry young.

Luckily, Tim, the man of her dreams, was a good choice.

Jill's feet, however, were firmly planted on the ground.

Suddenly she was aware that the child had reached her side and was now watching her mutely, waiting — but for what exactly? Silently, they walked the few yards to the car.

"Well, jump in!" She indicated the car.

He placed his bag carefully on the floor between his feet and fastened his seat belt, then he looked up at her with those wide brown eyes and smiled a little smile.

Jill felt a sudden pain in her chest, a deep ache. That smile. If the eyes were Jeannie's, then the wistfulness of the smile was all Tim's. They'd been such a close couple . . .

Tears blurred her eyes.

Now they were gone, Jamie was an orphan and Jill was the only thing standing between the little boy and foster parents or Care.

She still couldn't absorb the horrifying news that she'd lost her sister and brother-in-law. And of course, Jamie had lost both his parents.

Tim's uncle had taken Jamie as far as the first mainline station, then had put him on the right train for the next stage of his journey.

At his next change, the station manager had taken Jamie from one train to put him on the small branch connection which took him to where Jill would be waiting.

It had all gone without a hitch, but from the look on Jamie's pale little face, Jill imagined he'd been worrying the whole time.

SHE rounded a bend in the road and had to slam on the brakes. The road was full of sheep, a creamy, woolly sea of bouncing bodies.

Jamie perked up and looked out, a flicker of interest in his eyes.

"We'll have to wait," Jill explained, then she noticed Malcolm Strang standing by the wall.

She wound down the window and he bent and grinned in at them.

"And who is this? Friend of yours?"

"My nephew, Jamie Scott," she said. "He's coming to live with me at Bay Cottage."

"Hi there, Jamie," he said. "I'm Malcolm, but you can call me Malcolm!"

Jamie smiled.

Malcolm looked as if he'd like to know more, but there his questions ended.

"That was Malcolm Strang," Jill explained. "My cottage is next door to his farm."

Jamie nodded. He still hadn't said a word.

THEY reached the cottage and when Jamie got out of the car, he just stood and stared at it.

Jill wondered what he was thinking. Did it look grey and bleak to a sad little boy?

It was a rather ordinary cottage with a window either side of the porch and three dormer windows at the top, a far cry from the modern detached house on a large estate that Jamie was used to.

"Is that really all you have?" she asked, looking at his holdall. "There must be more. Toys?"

He shrugged.

"Well, come on in and I'll show you round." She kept her voice as cheerful as possible.

"Let's go upstairs first and you can see your room. It's at the back and you'll be able to see the river — and Malcolm's horses."

Jamie followed her up the narrow staircase. She opened the door to his room and wished she'd had time to make it nicer for him, although when he stepped in, his expression showed no emotion.

"We'll go into town and get some wallpaper, if you like. You can even choose some new curtains . . . Would you like that?"

He nodded.

"Well, why don't you get changed — put on some jeans and a

T-shirt, while I make some lunch. Do you like hot dogs? Chips? Chocolate mousse?"

Thank goodness for the village shop, Jill thought, as she tipped frozen chips into the basket and lowered it carefully into the fat.

She'd hardly had time to think of the impact this would have on her life. To be a globetrotting interpreter one minute and a mother the next.

There was so much to think of, not just feeding him and clothing him, but his emotional needs, too. That's where she feared she'd come unstuck.

She'd be able to see when he needed new shoes, but how would she tell when he needed a hug?

"Mind if I come in?"

"Oh, Malcolm, it's you," she said, startled.

"I did knock, perhaps you didn't hear."

"I was miles away."

He sat down at the kitchen table.

"So what's the story?"

"Jamie. He's my twin sister's son. She and her husband were killed in a car accident a few weeks ago."

She broke off and bit her lip. Would she ever get used to saying those words?

At that moment Jamie appeared in the doorway looking more relaxed in T-shirt and jeans.

"Hi." Malcolm grinned and held out his hand. "I hope you like living here, Jamie."

Jamie grunted something and shot a look at Jill.

Poor kid, she thought. Of all the people in the world, he had to be landed with an aunt he didn't really know!

The phone rang and she asked Malcolm to watch the chips while she hurried off to answer it.

Tim's uncle was calling to see if Jamie had arrived safely and to inform Jill that the solicitors would soon be in touch regarding the estate. She hadn't even thought of that!

The man waffled on for ages and by the time she got back to the kitchen, Malcolm had finished cooking the meal.

"It's coming to something," he complained, "when you invite yourself to dinner and end up having to cook it yourself!"

To Jill's surprise, Jamie giggled. It was a surprisingly nice sound and she found herself laughing, too.

"That was Uncle Harry on the phone," she said as she sat down. "Apparently they're having the rest of your things sent by carrier — your bike and stuff like that."

Jamie looked relieved, but said nothing. "Meg's had pups since you were last home," Malcolm announced.

"How lovely," Jill said.

Malcolm raised his eyebrows and jerked his head in Jamie's direction.

She coloured, wishing he'd stop before the boy noticed.

"Actually, they're all spoken for, bar one," he said.

"She's a bit on the small side and not so pretty as her brother and sisters, but kind of cute all the same."

Jill saw a spark of hope flame in Jamie's eyes, but the look she gave Malcolm was nothing short of deadly.

A S if I haven't enough to think about with Jamie, without you trying to land me with a wretched puppy," she blazed later, while Jamie pottered around in the garden.

"I was just thinking the kid needs something to love."

"I might not be Mother Of The Year material, but I'll take care of him."

"But will you love him?" Malcolm asked.

The look she gave Malcolm made his expression soften and he put his hands on her shoulders.

"I didn't mean that to sound the way it did. Of course you'll love him. What I mean is, will you let it show?

"You must, Jill!"

L ater, she stepped outside and saw Jamie perched precariously on the field gate with Malcolm keeping him steady.

"That's Bonny and the white one is Beauty." Malcolm was pointing out his horses.

"Do you have names for all your sheep, too?" Jamie asked, and Jill realised it was the first time since his arrival she'd heard him say a whole sentence.

"Of course I do," Malcolm said. "There's Lucy and Brightwell and Marjorie and Claire — oh, and there's a really grumpy one called Jillian."

"Watch your step, Strang!" Jill said. "I happen to know Jillian well and she's a lovely sheep."

Malcolm kept sheep only for their wool, horses for his riding school and goats because they were fun and he liked them.

He was, Jill thought, a thoroughly nice man, a man she could so easily fall in love with.

S he looked down at Jamie and held out her hand. For a terrible moment it seemed he would snub her, but his little hand reached out and found hers.

"What do you think?" she asked, her voice trembling. His hand felt so little in hers, but so trusting.

"Could we cope with a puppy?"

Jamie nodded vigorously.

"I think that's a yes," Malcolm said. The pup looked odd but cute and despite being the smallest little oddity, she was bright and healthy looking.

Jamie adored her.

"Well, that seems to be settled," Jill said.

She looked up and saw Malcolm was watching her extremely intently.

Could he feel, as strongly as she, the winds of change blowing through their lives?

"I'll tell you what," he said. "I'll keep her here for you until you get the cottage straight. I'll even help if you want any decorating done."

Jill looked down at Jamie. She was about to say they'd manage, but Malcolm had a way with the boy — and a way with her, too.

Maybe it was time to let the wind blow, see what change it brought with it and then wait for the dust to settle.

"Thanks," she said. "We'd like that, wouldn't we, Jamie?"

Jamie nodded.

They walked home across the field without speaking and she could sense him pulling away from her again.

The puppy wasn't going to be a solution by any means, but her presence would help, give them a starting point.

"So, you have a bike," she remarked. "Perhaps I could get myself a bike and we could go riding together."

"I . . ." He cleared his throat. "I used to go riding with my dad."

"Did you, love?" she said.

He stopped in his tracks and turned to face her.

"You look like my mum," he said, and his chin began to wobble.

"The boy's just like you, by all accounts. He hasn't shed a single tear since it happened. He's made of strong stuff, that's for sure," his uncle had said.

And she'd thought then, no, you've got it all wrong! It's all an act, a front! I'm human and vulnerable underneath — and so is little Jamie.

She fell to her knees in front of him and held out her arms to him.

"That's it, my love," she said gently, as he sobbed against her shoulder. "Let it all go, let it go."

Hugging him, holding him, seemed like the most natural thing in the world. It was easy and wonderful and she knew it would be the first of many such hugs.

She'd save her own tears for later and when they'd gone, when they'd passed, she'd start storing up the joy.

When Jamie finally moved away, there was a smile lurking in the tears and she kissed him, loving him and showing it.

Blow wind blow, she thought, do your worst for from this day on, things can only get better.

And somewhere, a long way away, she heard Malcolm whistling to his horses and for the first time in her life, she knew she was home. ∎

The Whole Truth

by Ann Monks

He cared deeply about Alison. Yet he knew she would never be his until he unlocked the secrets of her past . . .

THINK you're making a mistake," Graham had said and immediately wished he hadn't. He'd said it so many times he knew Alison had stopped listening.

She'd made up her mind, and once Alison embarked on something, she saw it through to the very end.

No matter what the consequences, Alison had been determined to find her real mother.

★★★★

"She mightn't want to see you," Graham had said when she'd first told him.

He knew he was being cruel but his motives were unselfish. He was trying to stop Alison getting hurt.

She was so special to him.

He'd written that once on a card to her, not long after they'd met.

He'd wanted to write I love you, but it had been too early in their relationship, so he'd put, To a special person, instead.

Alison had asked him round for a meal soon afterwards and his card had been prominently displayed on her mantelpiece.

"So, I'm rather special, am I?"

He'd thought she was teasing him and had smiled. But her next words had shocked him.

"I don't like being called 'special'."

He'd felt that, somewhere in her past, there was a reason for her dislike of that word.

But Graham knew when to pursue something and then was not the time or place. So he'd let it drop. If it was really important, it would come up again.

★★★★

And he'd been right. It had resurfaced the evening he'd invited Alison back to his place.

She'd wandered around his living-room, picking up books and ornaments, looking at the pictures on the walls, and had finally stopped at the array of family photographs.

Graham had identified his brothers, sisters and parents for her.

"You've got a big family, haven't you?" she'd said. There was a wistfulness about her that he hadn't seen before.

"Yes," he'd said. "What about you?"

The silence had hung between them for a while, then, keeping his tone as light as possible, he'd ventured, "You've never told me about your family . . ."

He'd waited, praying he'd made the right decision in pressing the matter. His gamble had paid off.

"Which one would you like me to tell you about?" Alison had asked.

"How many have you got?"

"Only the two," she'd replied.

"That's more than most people." He'd tried to make a joke of it.

"Actually, it's a lot less," she'd said. "I'm adopted."

A ND she'd told him that night all about her adoptive parents and her happy childhood and what she knew about her real mother, which wasn't very much. She'd also made it very clear she didn't want to discuss it again. Graham had respected her wish.

It was only when she'd taken him home to meet her parents that he'd dared broach the subject with her adoptive mother, Catherine.

Catherine had sighed, "From the day we told Alison she was adopted, she's refused to discuss it. We couldn't love her more if she was our own child, but it's as though part of her is locked away."

Catherine had gently touched his arm. "Try to be patient and have faith in her, Graham. It will all work out in the end."

And Graham had tried to believe that it would. He'd put it to the back of his mind and carried on with living life to the full with Alison.

After a year, they'd moved in together.

Things were almost perfect between them except for that no-go area, and Graham simply avoided it.

If Alison didn't want to talk about it, it didn't matter. They could still be happy together.

And they had been until the day he'd asked her to marry him.

"Don't you think you're rushing things?" Alison had said.

"Don't you love me?" Graham had retorted.

"Yes, of course I do," Alison had replied. "But I don't know if I'm ready."

"When will you be ready?" Graham had expected Alison to answer straight away and her answer had shocked him.

"When I've found my real mother," she'd said.

"But why bring that up now?" he'd asked.

"I can't tell you," Alison had answered. "Not till I find her."

They had had their first big argument then, and more had followed, and all about the same thing.

And so this woman whom they'd never even met was effectively driving a wedge between them.

SO Alison had left, only minutes before, closing the door quietly behind her. "Just be patient, Graham," she'd pleaded. "It will all be resolved soon. I'm very close to finding her." And then she'd gone.

Shortly after, the phone rang. Alison's words were still in his ears as he picked it up and heard the unfamiliar female voice on the line.

"May I speak to Alison Cavendish please?" The caller said the name as though it was strange to her.

"I'm sorry," he said. "She's not here. May I take a message?"

There was a pause and then the woman said, "No, I'll ring back."

Graham knew he should have just put down the phone, but, for some reason, he heard himself asking, "Are you Alison's mother?"

"Who is this?"

"I'm Graham Hamilton, Alison's boyfriend." He hesitated, wondering how much to say and then rushed on, "Alison and I are getting married.

"I'd like to come and see you." He stopped and then hurried on, "before you meet Alison."

Graham held his breath, certain she would refuse.

The woman's answer surprised him. "Very well, Graham."

She lived only an hour's drive away and it struck Graham that, all this time she'd been so close to Alison and they'd neither of them known it.

Graham drove past the house and parked farther down the road. He wanted to gather his thoughts but, no matter how he tried, he kept coming back to his irrational dislike of this woman, over and over again.

He blamed her entirely for the trouble between himself and Alison.

Yet, when he arrived at the address, it was such an ordinary house, it could have belonged to anybody.

HE was looking at a replica of Alison, some years older but with the same brown eyes and finely-shaped face.

How could he love one and hate the other?

"I'm Joanne," she said, and showed him into the sitting-room.

There were family photographs on the mantelpiece, of babies, schoolchildren and students, all of them with those same brown eyes, and he realised with a shock that Alison obviously had brothers and sisters as well as a mother, whom she'd never met.

Graham struggled to find the words. "I suppose you're wondering why I wanted to see you?"

"No. I think I know why," Joanne said simply. "You want to persuade me not to see my daughter. It's what I would do myself," she went on. "It means so much change, doesn't it? Not just to Alison and me, but her adoptive family and —" she gestured towards the photographs "— and to mine."

"Why didn't you keep her?" he blurted out, knowing it sounded like an accusation but also knowing she'd been expecting it.

"Because there was no way I could. Twenty-five years ago, it wasn't acceptable to be a single mother. And I was only sixteen, hardly out of school uniform. My family would only help me if I had Alison adopted."

"You could have been in touch with her before now if you . . ."

"Really loved her?" She finished the sentence for him.

"When I gave Alison up, I gave up any rights I had."

She paused, reading his disbelief, and then went on slowly and carefully, "I had no real control over my decision. It was forced on me by my parents."

Why is she trying so hard to convince me like this? Graham couldn't help thinking.

He suddenly felt sorry for Joanne, trying to justify herself to a virtual stranger.

Her next words pierced him like a sword piercing armour.

"You're trying to do the same to Alison as my parents did to me!"

He stared at her, all his defences down.

Suddenly, he saw what she meant. By trying to stop Alison meeting her mother, however good his reasons, he was trying to control Alison's life just as her mother's life had been controlled.

Perhaps, if Joanne had been left to work out her problems herself, how different her life might have been.

Joanne waited, giving him time. She didn't speak until Graham looked up at her.

"What will you tell Alison?" she asked.

Graham had difficulty speaking. "I'll tell her everything you said."

"You could ask her why she wants to see me now."

"Is that important?" Graham asked.

"It is for her."

Graham looked at her, his thoughts and feelings in turmoil.

He'd come here determined to dislike this woman, but he couldn't.

Instead, he found a grudging, yet genuine, respect beginning to grow.

"Don't worry," Joanne said. "I won't try to take Alison away from you."

"I'm not worried about that," Graham said. "It's just that I love Alison and I don't want to see her hurt."

For a second, a memory swept across her face and he caught a glimpse of intense pain before she covered it up.

"Sometimes," she said, "you can't have love without pain."

THAT night, when he told Alison what he'd done, she sat, calm and still, hearing him out.

"It was the uncertainty I couldn't take." He knew he was trying to justify his actions.

"Yes, the not knowing is unbearable, isn't it?" Alison said, and Graham felt ashamed he hadn't been as strong as her.

"Then why didn't you try to find her before now?"

"I felt at first that, if she didn't want me, then it was better not to. All my life people have told me I'm special — Mum and Dad because they adopted me and then you — all the people I love really and who love me.

"Well, I told myself, if I'm so special, why did my real mother give me away?"

Suddenly, Graham understood the reason for Alison's single-minded determination — she needed to be in control of her life because once, a long time ago, when she'd been tiny and dependent on others, the one person who should have wanted her, didn't.

"Then you wanted us to be married and I knew, deep down, I did too, but I had to sort this out first."

Her pain tore at Graham's heart but she wouldn't let him speak.

"When I was small and Mum used to cuddle me and I'd feel warm and happy, I imagined my heart having this little space in it that couldn't be reached and I had to keep it like that, so my real mother could some day fill it with her love and then I'd be complete.

"I was frightened that, if we had children, there would be a tiny part of me always empty for them, just as it was empty for Mum."

Graham remembered Catherine's fear and knew her intuition had told her this.

He tried to speak but Alison hurried on.

"It's all right. I know that, whatever my real mother's feelings are for me when I meet her, they won't change anything.

"Mum never held anything back from me. It was she who really mothered me. I don't have just one mother, I have two."

Alison stopped, her eyes a little bright.

Graham waited, knowing she had to say it herself, just as she had to make the journey to meet Joanne alone. Then perhaps she'd be able to release her pent-up feelings.

"I can't change the past but I can change the future, and I need to know," she said.

"I think your real mother loves you," Graham said.

"Sometimes, I feel she does, too," Alison agreed.

And Graham knew Alison hadn't just been searching for her mother.

She had been looking for herself — for the person she truly was.

She still had a long way to go, but he could help her with his own very special love for a very special person. ■

Keep Him Safe

by Teresa Ashby

*In trying to protect her son, she'd
overlooked just how much she, too,
needed some tender loving care . . .*

LUCY ran and ran and didn't stop until she reached the headland. There, bent double, hands resting on her thighs, she fought and struggled to get her breath back.

"Robbie!"

The wild wind snatched her voice away, carried it off and tossed it contemptuously into the pounding waves. She tried again.

"Robbie!"

She sank to her knees, despair crowding in all around her. "Oh, God, Robbie," she sobbed. "Where are you?"

They'd been here in the summer. Then, Lucy had had to smear Robbie's pale skin with sunscreen.

He was just turned eight, with long skinny limbs and a mischief of freckles speckling his nose.

"I like it here," he'd told her, before bounding off across the sand with Sheba hot on his heels.

Dear Sheba. She'd already been middle-aged when Robbie had come along; a little collie cross with seal-pup eyes and a huge swishy tail. They'd been a team practically from day one.

Lucy looked out over the thrashing sea. The gulls had settled on an outcrop of rock and were facing the wind like silent sentries.

"Robbie, where are you?" The plea was wrung out of her, a strangled cry that surely couldn't be heard.

Then suddenly from beyond the shelter of some rocks, up popped a tousled head and a face bearing an expression caught somewhere between puzzlement and fear.

"Mum?"

"Oh, Robbie!" she sobbed as she scrambled over stones and rocks towards him.

She held him to her. "What are you doing down here?" she cried. "You know you're not supposed to come here on your own."

"I was looking for Sheba," he replied simply. Lucy swallowed. "Sheba's dead, love," she said softly. "I explained all that to you."

"But Mr Chambers says no-one dies. He said Sheba wasn't in the ground, but in heaven and I thought . . ." His voice trailed away wistfully. "I thought it was like heaven here in the summer and so did Sheba."

Lucy groaned. Mr Chambers! Since he'd taken over at the swimming club, Lucy had heard nothing else.

Everything Mr Chambers said was gospel truth, apparently. But then, Robbie had never known a man in his life before.

His father had been killed in an accident at work.

Jim had died not even knowing that Lucy was pregnant.

Robbie turned and looked back towards the beach and she saw tears shimmering in his blue eyes.

"I thought she'd be there," he whispered. "I really thought she would."

LUCY suggested a piggy-back ride home and for once he didn't protest that he was getting too old. He felt heavy, and her arms began to ache, but she didn't mind. She'd carry him round the world.

"Oh, no," Lucy whispered when she saw a tall, lean shape hurrying towards them. "That's all I need right now."

"It's Mr Chambers!" Robbie cried joyfully and began to squirm to be put down.

"Robbie!" Mr Chambers cried, as soon as he saw the little boy running towards him, and Lucy's anger bubbled up, threatening to boil over in a scalding flood as Robbie leapt at his teacher.

He swung him round and round and she felt her heart constrict with a fierce protectiveness. He had no right to let Robbie get so fond of him, no right at all.

"This is all your fault, Mr Chambers!" she said.

"My fault? How do you make that out?"

"Robbie was down here looking for Sheba," she explained shakily. "You told him she'd gone to heaven and he thought . . . he thought it was at the beach."

He looked mortified.

Running his fingers through his thick dark hair he muttered, "I'm sorry, I didn't think —"

"No, you didn't," Lucy cut in. "I suggest you consider the outcome a bit more carefully next time, before you go charging in with your meaningful advice! Come along, Robbie."

IT was a week later, while Robbie was at school, that Lucy hurried to answer the doorbell and found Mike Chambers standing on the doorstep.

"Yes?" she said coldly. She looked pointedly at her watch. "I've a lot of work to do."

"Work?"

"Yes, Mr Chambers, work. I take in typing and I also organise the local evening paper round."

"I'm sorry, I won't take up too much of your time. I was just . . . well, Robbie hasn't been to swimming club this week and I wondered . . ."

She lowered her eyes, masking her expression. "It's his punishment for going off like that," she mumbled. "No swimming, no judo and no computer club after school for a fortnight."

She looked up at him.

"Aren't you going to tell me I'm wrong to punish him?"

"Not at all. Why, do you think you're wrong?"

"It seems so cruel when he was motivated by grief." The words were out before she could stop them.

"Have you considered getting another dog? Only my sister's dog has just had pups. They're bitzers of course, but very nice — bags of character."

69

"Bitzers?" She frowned, puzzled.

He grinned, and for a moment Lucy could see just why Robbie was so taken with this man. He certainly had charm.

"A Bitzer's a mongrel."

Lucy looked blank.

"You know, bitzer this and bitzer that — so, Bitzers!"

This time Lucy couldn't contain her laughter.

Maybe Mike Chambers wasn't so bad after all. Certainly, he couldn't be all bad if Robbie liked him so very much.

"Would you like a coffee?" she asked him.

"Thanks all the same, but I'm due at a lecture in ten minutes."

"A lecture?"

"In my spare time, when I'm not a swimming teacher, I'm an archaeologist. Strictly speaking, I'm Dr Chambers."

Lucy felt strangely sorry to watch him go, as he hurried back out to his car. It was, she suddenly realised rather sadly, the kind of car a family man drove. The kind that was usually packed to the roof with children, dogs and picnic baskets.

★★★★

The next time Lucy went to collect Robbie from his swimming lesson, she made a bee-line for Mike Chambers.

He was wearing his usual leisure centre T-shirt and blue tracksuit bottoms, and he looked, Lucy thought, really rather nice.

"Hello, good to see you again." He greeted her warmly, and there was no doubting the pleasure in his eyes.

"About the puppies," Lucy said, coming straight to the point. "I've been giving it a lot of thought and if it's still all right with you, Robbie and I would like to see them."

"Great!" He looked delighted. "If you've time, I'll drive you both to my sister's now. Polly won't mind."

Twenty minutes later, they arrived at Mike's sister's house. It was a vast Victorian place which was cluttered, untidy, and extremely welcoming.

"They're through here," Polly said.

Robbie knelt down at the edge of the makeshift pen as the puppies lumbered and scrambled towards him.

Lucy wanted this to be Robbie's dog and had already decided that as long as his choice was healthy and sturdy, she'd go along with it.

Almost at once, it was clear which of the pups was his favourite.

An appealing ball of fluff with cheeky black eyes and more energy than sense, nipped playfully at his fingers as Robbie stroked its head.

Tears welled in Lucy's eyes as her son cuddled and stroked the puppy. He looked sad as well as happy and she knew that he was thinking about Sheba, too.

"Can we have this one, Mum?"

Lucy nodded. "Yes, love. Of course we can."

JUST because we're getting Simba, it doesn't mean we don't love Sheba any more, does it?" Robbie asked, as Mike drove them home.

Tears burned at Lucy's eyes. She glanced across at Mike and shook her head. She was too full to speak.

Mike smiled gently, reassuringly, and cleared his throat. "You'll always love Sheba, Robbie," he said softy. "But love's a funny old thing. It just makes your heart grow and grow and there's always room for a bit more."

"So Sheba won't mind?"

"She'll be thrilled," Mike assured him. "She can't be here to look after you any more, so she'll be happy that Simba will.

"She'd be terribly unhappy if she thought you were still sad about her dying . . ."

Lucy closed her eyes. She knew that Mike wasn't just talking to Robbie about Sheba here. He was talking to her, too, about Jim — and he was right . . .

Since her husband had died, she'd more or less locked herself away, convinced that any attempt to make a new life for herself would be a betrayal of his memory.

But maybe that was being unfair to Jim's memory, she thought now. He'd never been a jealous or over-protective man. In fact, he'd been one of the most generous people she'd ever known.

Just what would he think of her caution, her insularity, now?

She already knew the answer. He'd be terribly anguished to think she was leading such a lonely existence.

If she closed her eyes, she could almost hear the warm lilt of his voice telling her to get out there and enjoy life.

She was still young and there were many times when she wished she had someone to lean on.

She glanced across at Mike and realised the car had stopped and he was staring at her.

"Can Mr Chambers stay for supper, Mum?" Robbie asked, bouncing around enthusiastically in the back of the car.

"Oh, I think Mr Chambers will want to get back to his own family," she replied, and his eyes, which had been regarding her so gently, suddenly filled with pain and confusion.

"But . . .!" Robbie protested from the back, and was silenced by Mike's low voice.

"It's all right, Robbie," he muttered. "I can take a hint."

Prickling all over with embarrassment, Lucy climbed out of the car and opened the back door for Robbie. A teddy bear rolled out with him and she retrieved it and handed it back to Mike.

"Better not leave him behind," she said, not quite steadily. "Your children would never forgive you."

He took the bear and at the same time, gripped her hand, his eyes locking with hers.

"I don't have any children," he said dryly. "Not yet anyway. I thought I might wait until I was married — always supposing I meet the right person, of course."

His eyes twinkled wickedly as a red hot flush filled her face.

"I thought . . ." she said hoarsely.

"This toy box on wheels is all thanks to my legion of nieces and nephews," he told her.

Robbie stood clutching her hand, looking from one to the other as if he were watching a tennis match, eyes wide, waiting for the next move.

"Does that mean Mr Chambers can stay for supper?" he asked at last.

"If Mr Chambers would like to," Lucy grinned.

"Mr Chambers is starving and would love to," Mike laughed and jumped out of the car. Then to Robbie he said, "And it's Mike, OK?"

"Mike!" Robbie beamed, delighted. "All right!"

As Robbie bounded ahead, a tangle of long arms and legs, Mike came alongside Lucy and reached for her hand, enclosing it in his, and leading her up the path.

"Not Uncle Mike?" she asked.

"Uncle's for my nieces and nephews," he said earnestly, and gave her hand a gentle squeeze. "I hope Robbie's going to be a bit more to me than that."

Her heart began to thud erratically as she stopped and turned to look at him.

"I — I'm not sure I . . ." she stammered. He smiled a gentle, loving smile, then bent his head and kissed her softly on the lips.

"I've wanted to do that since the first moment I saw you," he said. "I used to watch you bringing Robbie to the pool, then coming to collect him after the lesson.

"I think that must have been when I started to fall in love with you . . ."

Lucy gasped and he looked anxious, afraid he'd moved too quickly for her.

"I'm sorry . . ." he began.

"No," she said placing her finger against his lips. "Don't apologise. Kiss me again . . ." ■

After all those faithful
years, the time had finally
come for our old friend's last farewell . . .

"Goodbye, Snowdrop"

by June M. Hodges

73

COME quick, Mum." Sophie's little face, contorted with sobs, pleaded with me in the half-light as I opened the door. "Snowdrop can't get up."

It had finally arrived, the moment of truth.

Snowdrop was a 36-year-old pony, and he belonged to old Mr and Mrs Wilson who ran the local post office.

Sophie had been assigned to look after him and feed him for the past couple of years.

He lived about half a mile away, over the main road and across two or three fields, so Marianne, my elder daughter, or myself, always went with her to keep her safe. Marianne was with Sophie now.

When I saw the old pony desperately trying to hold his head up to eat his food, and teetering on tired old legs that refused to lift him, I knew.

Marianne knew, too.

And I think, deep down, that Sophie knew as well. I sent Marianne to the post office to tell the Wilsons to call the vet, and I knelt in the cold mud and held Snowdrop's head up to eat his last meal.

I kept my head down while tears fell on to his little pricked ears, and Sophie sobbed uncontrollably at my side.

"He's had a good life, Sophie. He's tired now, just tired."

Marianne came back and I told her to take Sophie home, that I would stay with Snowdrop until the vet came. She stroked him and said goodbye.

IT seemed an eternity that I was there, all alone in the bleak winter fields while darkness settled like a veil around us. I talked to Snowdrop, and stroked his face. He seemed serene, somehow, full of a beautiful peace.

The wind stirred the trees and lifted his mane. And very softly, without warning, it began to snow.

Silently, eerily, the large, swirling flakes fluttered on to his face and on to his long eyelashes, so that he opened his eyes and blinked.

Soon the darkness was a thick moving blanket that surrounded us, and there was just Snowdrop and me left in the whole world, clinging to each other in the white wilderness.

Please come soon, I prayed. The flakes were gentle and elegant, like flittering fairies.

What was I going to tell Sophie, I wondered. I knew that she understood a bit about death. She knew that it was final. For ever and ever. And that's what made it so hard.

And then they were all around me. From out of the speckled blackness they came, voices in the shifting night, drifting across the field.

I could hardly move my frozen hand to run it down Snowdrop's face.

"Well, this is it, old friend," I whispered. "I wouldn't have missed knowing you for the world."

Snowdrop blinked some white flakes off his eyes. I hoped he'd heard me.

Mr Wilson was puffing and harassed.

"Think old un's had enough," he said.

The vet put his hand on my arm. "OK, Mrs Jackson, you go home now. I'll see to him."

I was almost reluctant to leave. I wanted to see it through to the end. Wanted to be there when —

No I didn't! Who was I trying to kid? I wasn't that strong, I knew that.

So I hurried away, swallowed by the blizzard, leaving Snowdrop to the vet and Mr Wilson.

Numb with cold, and an awful emptiness, I ran across the last field, and the whirling, dancing fairies bore me home.

SOPHIE cried. And cried. And cried. She went to bed and sobbed into her pillow.

I sat beside her, and told her a story to try to comfort her. "A long time ago," I said, "before you were born, the fairies found a tiny little foal on a cloud.

"They decided to lend him to the Earth people for a while, so that he could enrich their lives and bring happiness to a lot of people. But only on the condition that when he was old and tired, the fairies would have him back again.

"When that day came, they said, they'd send a beautiful white winged stallion to escort him back up to the clouds. And he'd wear a glistening white robe of diamonds and there would be jewels in his mane."

Sophie stopped sobbing and listened, her eyes lighting up as the pictures formed in her mind.

"After he'd gone to sleep in the field, the snow came and made a blanket of diamonds. And then the moon came out, and the majestic stallion flew across it like a huge bird, and came down to the field to fetch the old pony.

"The fairies came, too, and threaded moonbeams through his mane and about his feet, so that he could be carried upwards. In the morning, he was gone, but the fairies had left the humans a gift, for taking care of him for all those years."

Sophie's eyes shone. "What? What did they leave?"

"Wait and see," I said. And together we went to the window, where a bright disc had sailed from the snow-clouds and lit the moonscape with silver.

As we watched, in awe of the spectacle, something swept across the moon, and dropped to Earth.

"Look! There he is!" Sophie cried. "The stallion!"

★★★★

The snow lay for weeks, in great frozen drifts at the side of the lanes.

After three days, I crept down to the field.

There was just a hole in the snow where he had lain, as if he really had been lifted by moonbeams.

I laid the little bundle of freshly-washed mane that I'd snipped from Snowdrop as he lay in my arms and tied with a pink ribbon on the frozen ground, and called at the post office on the way home.

"That 'elicopter came quick, couldn't get a vehicle down there in all that snow."

I smiled. Mystery solved. Snowdrop had, indeed, been spirited away into the sky, but by helicopter instead of fairy threads of moonbeams.

Sophie and I went down the next day and she squealed with delight at the ribboned bundle of mane that the fairies had left. And in that moment I knew that Sophie was all right. The fairy story had done the trick.

Soon would come the spring, with warm sunshine to chase away the shadows of winter and melt the memory of that icy night when Snowdrop had breathed his last.

WE went for a walk down to the field one Sunday afternoon in February.

Sophie ran across the field, flinging her arms wide to the purpling sky, embracing freedom and youth, enriched by her surroundings and the lingering memory of Snowdrop.

He was everywhere, all around us, in the wind and the sunlight and beneath our feet. Not in a sad way, but in celebration of a grand, full life and a wonderful friendship.

Suddenly, Sophie stopped and squealed. I went over. It was the exact spot where the old pony had lain on my lap, where his life had gently ebbed away while his eyes grew dim like blackened jewels gone far into the night.

And there, just in that one spot in the whole of the field, with their tiny heads bobbing in the breeze, was a scattering of snowdrops . . . ∎

The Daughter
I Never Had

by Joyce Begg

She made today *so* special for me —
although it was *her* wedding day . . .

The bride's late, although I expect it's the photographer's fault.
I hope Gordon's warm enough. I wonder if he thought to wear a
vest.

I must not be a fussy mother.

The boys — I mean the groom and best man — have appeared
now, so Lindsey can't be far behind. They do look smart. I'm glad they
agreed to wear kilts.

Although I shouldn't be the one to say so, Gordon does look

handsome. They both do. They're very presentable boys. Men, really.

After all, Gordon's 25. I suppose Dave must be much the same. He's working out in Sydney now, Dave.

I recognise the strains of Handel as we all struggle to our feet and wait for the bride's appearance.

The groom has turned and is beaming at Lindsey, obviously bursting with love and pride. Bless him.

I'm going to cry, blast it!

My eyes take in the details of the back of the dress, the neckline, the neat waist, the train, uncluttered and graceful. But my mind's suddenly far away, and I find myself thinking back over the years, back to the time Gordon first brought Lindsey home.

There were still in school, barely 16. I thought then she was a funny-looking kid, her hair sticking up in ribbons, a frivolity at odds with the scholarly glasses. But I liked her.

Sixteen or not, they were passionately in love right from the start. They did everything together; went to discos, played music, did their homework. They even watched telly from the same beanbag.

They weren't always on their own, of course. There was a gang of them, all great friends. I think Dave was on the fringes of that group.

But whoever else was with them, they were always acknowledged as a couple. Gordon and Lindsey. Lindsey and Gordon.

THEY both went away to university — the same one, of course. I remember questioning the wisdom of this.

"Shouldn't you be going to different places?" I had the temerity to ask. "You do want to meet other people, don't you?"

But I was wasting my breath. I had to be satisfied with the fact that they were doing different courses and would spend probably less time together than they had in the past.

I was also assured that the university they had chosen was the best one for their individual requirements.

So, although I was worried that they might become too dependent on each other, I accepted their logic and let them get on with it.

It was during their second year that Lindsey's father was promoted and the rest of her family moved south. After that, our home became her base.

You don't always see the changes in your own youngsters, but I watched Lindsey change from a rather awkward teenager into a very appealing young woman.

Then there was the time that Gordon came back on his own. "Couldn't Lindsey make it this time?" I asked.

"I've no idea what Lindsey's doing," he said, and went off to his room.

A FEW weeks later, we got the panic phone call. "Mum, can I bring Lindsey home? She's ill."

"Yes, of course you can. What's wrong with her?"

"She was feeling rotten and went to the university doctor. He said she was to go home and be properly looked after, but she can't."

"She can't what?"

"She can't go home," he said impatiently. "Her folks are in America. They're away for a month."

It was mumps.

Gordon brought her back on the train, almost carrying her from the carriage to the car.

They came on a Friday. Gordon spent the whole weekend running up and down stairs, taking her drinks, holding her hand. I'd never seen him so worried.

On Tuesday, I sent him away with words of reassurance.

"You can't afford to miss any more classes. Lindsey will be fine.

"You've been a great help, but what she needs now is just to be left on her own. Peace and quiet. I expect she'll sleep quite a lot."

"Are you absolutely sure? Because I couldn't bear it if . . . I just couldn't bear it."

So that was them back together again. Illness had made them realise how much they meant to each other, whatever their disagreement had been about. Their attachment was more intense than ever.

My own affection for Lindsey was stronger, too. I really did feel she was becoming the daughter I never had.

And although her own mother was, naturally, much dearer to her than I was, I know Lindsey also felt the bond between us.

Which is one reason why I'm finding this particular wedding so difficult.

Who'd have thought that after all that, Gordon and Lindsey would in time outgrow each other, that their paths would separate, although they still remained friends?

Who'd have thought that the strong, silent Dave, Gordon's close companion in later years, would fall so much in love with Lindsey that he'd go to Australia to avoid the pain, only to step in to claim her from a distance of 12,000 miles, when she and Gordon split up.

The wedding party are returning from the signing of the register. The organ is thundering out Mendelssohn, and the happy couple beam radiantly at everyone as they proceed down the aisle.

As Lindsey passes, she stops at our pew and lightly kisses my cheek. She must have tasted my tears.

Behind her, comes the best man, who pats the bridesmaid's hand, and winks in my direction. A young man with a happy heart and no regrets. My son, Gordon. ■

For them, he'd filled the garden with
goodness and beauty and memories.
Now it was time to repay the debt . . .

Harry's Gift

by Ann
Monks

JEAN frowned as she looked down the garden; the weigela was late flowering this year. It had always been one of the pleasures of spring that she looked forward to, and somehow being able to see its avalanche of soft pink flowers made the task of washing-up less of a chore.

She sighed. If it didn't hurry up, she wouldn't see it bloom.

For a moment, her vision blurred with unshed tears and she made herself stare down hard into the bowl of soapy water.

Get a grip on yourself, woman! The small voice inside her that had coaxed her through moments like this since Harry had gone, came to the rescue again.

Fancy getting sentimental about a shrub. Why, there were far more important things in life than plants.

A rueful smile caught at her lips as she remembered when she'd said the same thing to Harry. It had been forty years ago almost to the day.

They'd stood on the back doorstep of this house and stared out at what had looked like a sea of mud.

It had been raining all night — their first night in their new home — and the topsoil the builders had spread over the rubble of the building site had been pitted with huge puddles.

The house had been cold and damp. All they'd had was the bed in which they'd curled up together, and a couple of chairs and a table.

Jean hadn't minded, though, not as long as she had Harry. At least, she hadn't minded until he'd started to talk about how he was going to lay out the garden.

"Well, I want some kitchen cupboards before you go planting roses," she'd said.

"I'll make you a beautiful kitchen," he'd replied. "But surely you want something lovely to look out on."

"I'll be too busy to have time to look out the windows!"

Harry hadn't said anything to that. He'd just smiled.

She'd been so impatient in those days to have everything right straight away, but Harry wouldn't be hurried.

"We've got the rest of our lives ahead of us," he'd say. "Plenty of time to do things. Let's enjoy ourselves."

He'd made her the kitchen cupboards, but he'd also sown a tiny lawn. She'd bridled a bit at that.

"That's not the best place for my washing line," she'd said, as she'd watched him move it to the side of the house. "I won't get nearly as much sun or wind on it there."

"Ah, but you can't sit out on a washing line," Harry had replied. "And the kids can't play out on one, either."

"We haven't got any kids," she'd said, and again Harry had just smiled.

SHE'D remembered her words the following year when little Tom had crawled for the first time across the smooth grass that Harry had carefully tended.

That was all there was in the garden then, that and the three borders of bright annuals that somehow Harry had managed to conjure up from nowhere.

Harry hadn't had much time for gardening, either. He'd worked long hours all through that autumn to buy Tom's pram and cot.

The following spring, he'd dug over the bottom half of the garden and planted potatoes in long rows.

Jean had looked out at the dark earth.

"Aren't we going to have any flowers this year?" she'd asked. "I've got nothing to look out at."

And Harry had just smiled.

He'd called her outside the next day. There had been a fine mist of rain and everywhere was wet.

Jean had pulled a face. She'd only just put Tom down after his midday feed and she had a pie to make for tea, as well as a long list of chores. Coming out into a cold April day was the last thing she'd wanted to do.

"I need your help," Harry had insisted. "Come on, I can't do this on my own."

So, reluctantly, she'd followed him out. Beneath the back kitchen window, Harry had dug a hole and in it he was supporting what looked to Jean like a prickly, dead twig.

"You can do the honours this time," he said, nodding towards the spade that leaned against the side of the hose.

Reluctantly, Jean started to shovel in the soil.

"Go carefully," Harry had said as she'd let a large clod fall on to the fragile roots. "Just stop for a minute."

He'd leaned down and crumbled the earth with one hand, whilst the other supported the tree and then, ever so gently, he'd spread it evenly about its roots, patting it down, just as though he'd been tucking a blanket round Tom.

"You've got to give things a good firm foundation otherwise they won't last a lifetime," he'd said.

Jean had been more careful then. She still hadn't been very keen on being out here in the cold rain when she had so much to do.

To her, making a hot pie for tea had been a lot more important than planting what looked like a dead branch, but she could tell that it had mattered to Harry and so it mattered to her.

"So what is it?" she'd asked, as she'd watched Harry firm the last spadeful around the bare-branched tree.

"You'll just have to wait and see, won't you?" he'd said with his usual smile, and the complaint that he had dragged her away from something equally important had vanished from Jean's lips before she could voice it.

Jean had waited all through the spring, watching the seemingly-dead branches throw out small green buds and the buds unfold into small green leaves.

"I know what it is," she'd said to Harry one day. "It's a rose bush."

"Top marks!" Harry had laughed at her.

She'd thrown a cushion at him. "I'll make a good gardener one day," she'd said.

"One day maybe," Harry had replied contentedly.

Harry had given her something to look at though, from her kitchen window. The rose they planted together bore ten blossoms that year. One for every month of little Tom's life.

It had been a fine, hot August when she'd looked out the kitchen window and watched another pale pink flower open itself to the sun, each petal softly gilded with a sheen of gold.

Beneath it, tucked into the earth, was a small wooden sign on which Harry had carved, Tom, 1953, 'Dearest'.

"Why 'Dearest'?" Jean had asked.

"It's the name of the rose, love."

Jean hadn't even known that rose varieties had different names. She'd been brought up in a dark terraced house with a back yard, and the only plants she had seen had been the weeds that strained for light between its flags.

Money was scarce then, before the war, and so hard to earn that it was spent very carefully.

Jean supposed that's where her serious attitude towards life had started. It was a habit she'd found almost impossible to change.

When she left school and went to work in a shop, she'd carefully planned how to spend every single penny she earned as wisely as possible.

When her friends wanted to go dancing or to the cinema, Jean had to be coaxed along.

Her very best friend Margaret had lost patience with her one day.

"Honestly, Jean, I wish you'd be less serious. There's more to life than work, you know."

Against her will and more to stop Margaret from scolding her, Jean had finally agreed to go to a dance.

She'd met Harry that night and had refused every dance with him and everyone else who had asked her. But Harry had kept coming back, again and again.

She was to remember his persistence and also his smile — a soft, gentle smile that didn't tease her or mock her for being so serious.

She hadn't known why she'd gone back the following week, but she had, and this time she'd danced with him. But it was a month before she'd let him walk her home.

★★★★

"Oh, yes, Harry, you were certainly the patient one," Jean murmured now, staring down the length of garden towards the vegetable plot.

It was what made Harry such a good gardener. She remembered the time she'd wanted potatoes for their tea.

"Surely they're ready now?" Jean had queried that first year.

"Nope! They'll be no bigger than pigeons' eggs," Harry had replied and refused to dig up a tuber. "Just give 'em another ten days and you'll have a good panful."

It had all been a mystery to Jean, this having to wait for the potatoes to be ready when she'd been so used to getting hers from the greengrocer's.

Harry had been proved right, though, and the flavour of those first potatoes from their own garden would remain with her forever. So much so, that the following year when she'd seen Harry digging up the potato patch to plant beans, she had demanded to know what he was doing.

"You've got to give the earth a rest, Jean. You can't expect it to keep on working on the same thing forever," he'd replied. "Otherwise it gets tired."

He'd said something else as well, about crop rotation, but Jean had been too busy thinking about his first words to bother with all the technical nonsense — that had been for Harry to think about.

The following day, when she'd put Tom down for his afternoon nap, Jean had left her duster in the cupboard instead of cleaning everywhere as she usually did.

Instead, she went out and carefully and gently planted all the bedding plants Harry had grown from seed. By the time Tom woke up, she'd done all three borders round the lawn.

She couldn't wait for Harry to come in to see her handiwork. All through tea-time she wished he'd hurry and finish. When finally he pushed his plate away and got up to go for his usual tour of the garden, she'd followed him to the back kitchen door.

He'd stood there staring in silence and then he'd looked at her.

"Been doing a bit of gardening?"

"Don't you like it?" Jean had peered over his shoulder. Her rows of flowers were straight and neat, as spick and span as her polished, shining house.

"It looks very nice," Harry said and then added, "At the moment, at least . . ."

"What do you mean 'at the moment'?" Jean had found it hard to keep the indignation out of her voice.

"Well, you've put the alyssum and lobelia at the back of the row and the snapdragons at the front. One'll grow so tall you won't be able to see the other."

"Oh, no!" Jean had cried. "And it took me all afternoon to do."

Harry had held up a hand. "Don't worry. I'll soon put it right."

"But I wanted to help," Jean had told him. "It's not my fault they all look the same when they've no flowers."

Harry had smiled ever so gently at her and pulled her to him.

"You'll soon learn," he'd said.

He'd been right — she had.

By the time they'd replanted those borders together, Jean could tell a marigold from a lupin and a salvia from a sweet pea.

From then on, she'd spent more and more time in the garden, either just pottering about while Tom was asleep, or playing with him when he was awake.

One day when Margaret had called round and found her curled up next to Tom on his blanket on the lawn, she'd remarked on it.

"I never thought I'd see you out here, catching forty winks in the middle of the day."

"Why ever not?" Jean had replied, not admitting to having had the same misgivings that morning as she'd spotted the dust on the sideboard. "It's a lovely afternoon. It'd be such a waste to spend it inside."

The sun had been shining and Tom had wanted to play and she'd learned that housework could always wait.

They had been wonderful, those years. The children had come along and the garden had grown with them. The lawn had grown larger so Tom could kick a ball and when little Hazel was born, they'd bought a slide.

Harry had bought something else as well, a hazel tree, and he'd made a little sign to go beneath it just as he'd done for Tom. Robert had been the last to come along, almost eight years after Tom. He was a strong, sturdy baby.

"He's like a young oak tree," Harry had said, and when Jean had raised an eyebrow, he'd shaken his head. "It's all right, love, I'm not thinking of planting one of those. We'll get him a nice apple tree."

Jean could see it now, the last of the blossom on it barely visible. It had yielded fruit every year of its life, but this year she wouldn't be tasting the apples.

She picked up the kettle and filled it.

A cup of coffee was required, she decided, and when she'd made it, she took it outside to drink.

IT was a beautiful morning. This was the best time of year, Jean thought; her favourite time.

Everything was still young and new, like the first years of her marriage.

If she closed her eyes now she could swear she was back then, with Hazel making mud pies in the sandpit, Tom kicking his ball, and Robert trying to join in with his elder brother.

But the children were grown and had families of their own now, and the lawn had been mostly sacrificed to a long, herbaceous border. They'd put that in the day Robert had left home, the last of their children to fly the nest.

Margaret had come round to help her plant it, bringing cuttings and roots from her own garden.

Jean stopped by the tall, feathery astilbe, one of Margaret's favourites, and stroked its elegant blooms. Each year it flowered and each year she stroked it and thought of Margaret, her dear friend of a lifetime and the last time they'd stood here together.

"I'm going to miss you," Jean had told her.

"And I'm going to miss you, too," Margaret had replied. "You've been a good friend to me, Jean, but I'm lonely since Jack died. And the children want me to go out to them. I haven't seen my Jenny since Paul's wedding and Paul's wife is expecting their first child next year.

"You could come out and visit me, you and Harry."

It was such a long way, though, Jean had thought — Canada — the other side of the world. Such a long way from her little home and its garden, a tiny world in which she'd lived happily with Harry.

She walked on down the garden and stopped under the apple tree, the one Harry had planted for Robert. Already, she could see the tiny swelling of the fruit, rosy red behind the faded flowers.

It looked like it would be a good year for apples. She remembered Robert at four years old trying to climb the tree and being scolded by Harry.

"It's only a sapling still, you'll break it. You'll need to wait a few years yet, lad."

Well, it was strong enough now and Robert's son had climbed it last summer, while she'd hovered anxiously underneath.

She carried on a bit farther and paused at the gate to the vegetable garden. Everything was as neat and tidy as when Harry had been there to look after it.

The potatoes were growing as strong as ever. She might even be able to dig some up for tea.

She looked up at the sky, wondering if it would rain and whether she should do it now or later. Then her gaze turned to the hooks in the archway over the gate.

Harry had trained a climbing rose over it, after the children had stopped using the swing.

She'd been sorry to see it go. There was many a day she'd come down here and sat on it herself after she'd hung out the washing. The first time she'd done it, she'd felt silly, but it hadn't stopped her doing it again.

She'd laughed when she'd told Harry.

"I bet you never thought you'd see me on the children's swing."

And Harry had just smiled

She made her way along the flagged path up the side of the greenhouse. They were Harry's tomatoes growing there. The last seeds he'd planted. She didn't go in.

Tom would see to the greenhouse when he called in later. It had become his job since Harry had gone.

On the patio, the last of the lilies were flowering in the big stone pots Harry had filled. Hazel had carried the flowers in her wedding bouquet.

Jean bent her head now to draw in their scent, and memories of that happy day came flooding back.

And that's all they are now, Jean thought, as she turned to look at the garden. Just memories.

Harry had made this place beautiful and filled it with shrubs and vegetables and flowers — and with something else as well.

Now Jean couldn't stem the tears. She had known this year would be the hardest of all, the first year without him.

That was why Margaret had invited her for a holiday and why Jean had agreed to go.

"You'll be all right, Mum, and we'll look after everything for you. Don't worry, the garden will be fine," Tom had urged.

The children had been good. Robert came to cut the grass and Hazel insisted on pruning the roses. Everyone was busy in Harry's garden, everyone except her, and if she couldn't do anything in it now of all times, then all Harry's work over the years would have been for nothing.

She found herself standing in front of the old rose bush, the first one she'd helped Harry plant, and thought how he'd had to coax her out of the kitchen that rainy April day.

"But you wouldn't ever take no for an answer, would you, Harry?" she said. "You never gave up."

The first buds were forming on the rose. Jean touched them as gently as she'd once touched baby Tom's head. The little wooden sign that Harry had placed beneath it was long gone, but it didn't matter. Everyone in the family knew it was Tom's tree.

Dear Harry, Jean thought. He was always thinking about someone else and here am I just thinking about myself.

In two weeks' time she would be in Canada, staying with Margaret and her family for the summer.

When she'd agreed to go, she'd felt she was running away and dreaded the prospect of returning to the empty house in the autumn. But standing here, looking at Tom's tree, she knew how and why she would return, hard though it might be.

Exactly a week later, Jean stood back and surveyed her handiwork. She was glad she'd chosen this place; the herbaceous border had needed a good clean out and Harry had earmarked this year to do it.

Maybe he wouldn't have chosen to plant something at this time of year, but it wouldn't come to any harm. Tom had promised to give it a good watering every day, and when she returned in the autumn, she'd replant a smaller border around it.

There would be so much to do to get the garden ready for the following spring, not just for herself but for her grandchildren, too. Harry had made it a garden for people and she would carry on where he'd left off.

There was a new swing to buy and she'd get Tom and Robert to build another sandpit on the patio to replace their old one, which had been filled in all those years ago.

Reducing the size of the border would give more lawn for Robert to kick a ball with his son. She was sure Harry would approve of what she was doing — indeed of what she had just done.

She kneeled down now to smooth the soil around the trunk of this latest addition to the garden and looked up through its slender fledgling branches at the sky. Somewhere up there she knew Harry was watching.

He'd planted something for everyone, but never for himself.

She pushed the little wooden sign she'd made securely into the soil. She was rather proud she'd known exactly which tree should be Harry's; not bad for a girl who once hadn't known that plants had names — but then no other tree would have done.

"It's just right, isn't it," she murmured as she read the inscription. "Harry, 1994, 'Tree of Heaven'." ◼

A New Tomorrow

by Sally Woods

Once before, she'd loved a little boy. Had she the courage now to open her heart to another?

TRY as she might, Carrie couldn't get little Jason out of her mind. He was a lovely little boy, with blond, unruly hair that seemed to be forever falling in his eyes.

Liz, a friend of the family, as well as being a social worker, had talked Carrie into meeting Jason.

"Ach, Carrie — he's a wee angel!" Liz had said.

Yet, when Liz had introduced them, it took a long time for Jason to respond to Carrie's handshake.

Then, suddenly, he'd returned her smile and it was like the sun coming out.

That smile of his had gone straight to her heart — but it had disappeared again as quickly as it had come.

All the same, it had stayed long enough for Carrie to know that, behind it, this shy little boy had been hoping she would like him.

Only, Carrie didn't really want a Jason. She didn't want any little boy. Little boys brought back too many sad memories. She wanted a little girl.

Carrie's own two daughters were grown up now and away from home and she missed them terribly.

She had far too much time on her hands now, time that could be very well spent, if she took on what she had been thinking about for ages — if she went in for long-term fostering.

She had talked the idea over with David, her husband, and he had agreed with her that it was a wonderful idea.

"But I'm not taking on a boy!" Carrie had been very definite about that. "I couldn't," she'd told him. "Not after Mark."

"No-one will ever replace Mark," David had said in his quiet, kind way. "Just in the same way no-one could ever take the place of our daughters."

Carrie had felt the familiar prick of tears at the back of her eyes. "But it's different," she'd protested. "After all, our daughters are still alive. Mark is . . ."

"It's all right, love. Don't upset yourself. A little girl it is then," David had said.

Even thinking of that recent scene made Carrie shed a few tears again as she remembered their little Mark. He had died five years ago, when he was only four years old.

The doctors said he'd had a hole in his heart which had gone undetected when he was born.

David, herself and their two daughters had been devastated — he had been such a loving child.

It was as if, looking back, he had been trying to distribute enough love in his four short years to last them a lifetime.

It had taken Carrie a long time to come to terms with losing Mark, if she really had. Even yet, there were still days when she just wanted to sit down and cry for him.

Their attic was still full of his toys. There were the toy tractors and cars he had been so fond of, his teddy and his picture books.

She knew that, someday, she would have to get rid of them. But not yet.

NOW this other little boy — this Jason, with his shy smile and wayward hair that fell over his eyes — had suddenly come into her life.

All of a sudden, she was feeling angry with him.

She told herself she was being unkind and unreasonable but his solemn little face was obscuring her image of Mark.

Suddenly, she made up her mind — she wasn't going to think about this any more.

She still had to make the curtains for the bedroom they had decided to redecorate for the little girl they were hoping to foster.

Carrie began to spread the material she had bought for the curtains out on the kitchen table.

By the time she had finished, the room was going to bring a delighted smile to some little girl's face.

Carrie paused, the scissors poised over the material.

Maybe she should meet with Jason just one more time?

After all, if her little Mark had still been alive and in need of a good stable home . . .

No! No, she couldn't even think about it!

Perhaps if she met him on her own, without Liz's influence?

If she met him on her own, she might find that they didn't really suit each other. Then that would be that — there would be no question of taking him home to live with them.

This was no use — she had to phone Liz!

Quickly, before she could change her mind, she went straight to the phone. "Liz? It's me, Carrie!" she said. "Look, I was wondering, would you arrange it so I could meet Jason again?"

There was a short pause, then Liz said slowly, "All right, if you're sure you want to?"

"I'm not sure about anything, any more," Carrie replied with a sigh. I keep thinking, if it was my little Mark needing a home . . ." Her voice tailed away. "What am I going to do, Liz?"

"I can only say this — little Jason needs someone very badly and I can't help thinking you could be that someone."

"Liz, do you think I could meet him on my own this time? I just feel it would be better."

"I'm sure that will be no problem," Liz said. "I'll see what I can do and phone you back as soon as I've arranged something."

It was the next day before Liz phoned back. "Can you be at the park gates at, say, three o'clock?"

Carrie waited by the park gates until nearly ten past three. Then she saw Jason climbing out of Liz's car. Liz wound down the window and shouted, "Sorry we're late! I was delayed just as we were about to leave."

Carrie hardly heard her — her eyes were on Jason.

His fringe was over his eyes again and that made a lump come to her throat.

When Mark's hair had needed cutting, it used to do the same thing, only Mark's hair had been dark and not nearly as thick as Jason's.

Jason was staring at her, very seriously. It was almost as if he was reading her thoughts.

Carrie mentally shook herself. As if he could. He was only a little boy. He knew nothing about Mark.

"Hello, Jason," she said softly.

"Hello," he answered quietly, smiling just long enough for Carrie to read again the unspoken message she was sure she had glimpsed the first day they met. He really wanted her to like him. She felt her heart reach out to him.

They strolled aimlessly through the park, Carrie not speaking very much. Yet, somehow, there was nothing uncomfortable about that.

She hadn't taken his hand. Part of her wanted to, but there was a lump in her throat every time she thought about it. It would be much too painful to take Jason's hand.

Then, all of a sudden, without warning, she felt his small hand slip into hers.

Carrie looked down at him.

He was looking up at her.

He smiled at her, his little face and his eyes crinkled up against the weak November sun.

She took him to see the ducks. One of them was swimming around the pond at a terribly fast rate. It was skimming in and out amongst the rest of the ducks, sending them into frenzied quacking.

Jason was greatly taken by this. He kept pointing excitedly.

Then, to Carrie's amusement, he went into a fit of the giggles.

It was the first time she had heard him laugh and it was such an infectious sound that she found herself giggling along with him.

Then, all of a sudden, Liz was coming towards them and Carrie realised their time was up.

It was time to hand Jason back and, to her surprise, she was swamped with acute disappointment.

Liz called out, "Hello, you two!" She was smiling at them, but her smile had an anxious edge to it.

Jason didn't seem to want to let go of Carrie's hand. He was staring up at her, his anxious eyes fixed on Carrie's, waiting.

His fringe had tumbled forward to meet his eyes again.

Carrie reached down and did what she had been longing to do since they'd first met.

She pushed that unruly fringe of his back from his forehead.

She bent down in front of him and put her arms around him. She held him while a tear trickled down her face.

Jason put out a tiny finger and touched it. Then, he said the longest sentence he had said yet. "You don't want me, do you? It's all right. Don't cry."

"Oh, Jason. Oh, sweetheart!" Carrie cried. "I do want you. I want you so much! And so does my husband, David."

She held him tighter, until the tears stopped coming.

Then she looked up at Liz and said, "Is it all right if David and I collect Jason first thing in the morning?" while asking herself how she could ever have thought of not having him "He's coming home to live with me and David. Aren't you, Jason?" she added, smiling down at him.

Carrie had straightened up and Jason looked up at her, his eyes wide.

He never said a word, but his small arms wrapped themselves tightly around her knees as he gave her a fierce hug.

Carrie pushed his hair away from his eyes again. "See you tomorrow, Jason," she said, smiling.

She watched as he and Liz walked away.

He had hold of Liz's hand now. But he kept looking back over his shoulder and waving at her, and his smile lit up his whole face.

Carrie didn't go straight home, though she was desperate to tell David everything. She knew he'd be delighted.

Instead, she hurried towards the shops.

That curtain material was no use at all for a boy's room. She would put it aside for, you never knew, maybe it would come in useful sometime.

For now, she would buy something Jason would like.

And she would take down all those toys from the attic — the tractors, the cars, and all the things that had belonged to Mark.

She could imagine Mark pushing them over to Jason to play with.

And she could still see Mark's big smile and his straight, dark hair and she knew at last that nothing, absolutely nothing, could ever take that away from her. ■

He was only looking for a clean shirt. He certainly didn't expect to uncover his wife's deepest secret!

What A Surprise!

by Teresa Ashby

THINGS like this hadn't happened when he'd been living at home with his parents. Every morning his mother would wake him up with a cup of tea and by the time he got up, there'd be a neat pile of clothes waiting for him at the end of his bed.

"I thought helpless men went out with flared trousers!" Anthea quipped, laughing at his hopeless expression. "Why don't you look in the linen cupboard? There's bound to be a shirt in there for you to iron."

"Me?" he said, going pale. "Iron?"

"Up to you," she said, grabbing her bag and keys and heading for the door. "Either iron a shirt or go to work with your chest on show."

"Couldn't you just . . . ?" he called, as she slammed the door behind her.

"I'm a 'new man'," he went on in a whisper to the empty flat. "I cry at sad films and help with the shopping. What more do you want?"

There was a clean but crumpled shirt in the linen cupboard, but as to where she kept the iron . . .

They'd only been married a year — no-one could expect him to know where everything was.

He knew they had an iron because he'd seen her using it — usually late at night when they both realised they had nothing to wear the next day.

It was strange she hadn't realised he hadn't any shirts left, last night . . .

He checked her wardrobe for the iron. . . and nearly fainted.

Why on earth would she keep a baby bath in her wardrobe? Unless . . . He hardly dared check any further, but knew he must.

Blimey! She had a whole range of baby stuff in there from disposable nappies to cotton buds.

There was a white all-in-one suit, the kind that made babies look like wind socks, some vests with big necks and some tiny little socks.

He sank down on to the bed and held a soft little teddy against his cheek.

"She's having a baby," he murmured dreamily. "Why didn't she tell me?"

Then he looked down at his still-shirtless chest and knew precisely why she hadn't told him.

He was useless — that was why! He couldn't iron a shirt, cook a potato, or clean the bath.

The poor girl was probably terrified at the thought of bringing a child into the world knowing he'd give her all the support of a long-perished rubber band.

Quickly, neatly, he packed all the baby stuff back into her wardrobe and felt an uncontrollable urge to laugh out loud in the rising tide of his excitement.

"A baby," he said happily.

He could just see himself strolling through the park pushing along one of those natty little prams. But there was no time for day-dreaming . . . he had to find that iron!

Eventually he found it and the ironing board behind the kitchen door.

However, after a long struggle with the board, he gave up and spread a towel on the worktop.

Ironing wasn't as easy as Anthea made it look.

He burned his fingers twice and scorched an iron-shaped mark on his shirt, but was so encouraged by the end result, he went through the whole linen cupboard, ironing everything.

HE was home from work first and already cooking dinner when she came in.

Love welled up inside him. She looked weary, but, of course, she was bound to.

"Sit down," he urged, leading her to a chair. "Put your feet up. Dinner will soon be ready."

She refused to stay seated and followed him into the kitchen in a bemused kind of way.

"You did all the ironing," she gasped in complete amazement.

He consulted the open cookery book on the draining-board and turned down the heat under a pan.

"You're using the cooker!"

"Sit down, sweetheart. Would you like a drink?"

"I certainly need one, after this . . ." Then her tone changed to suspicion.

"What have you done?" she asked, warily.

"Well, I dusted a bit when I got in, then I peeled the potatoes and carrots and set the table . . ."

"No," she said, "I mean what have you *done?* You're obviously feeling guilty about something. And what happened to your shirt?"

He looked down at the brown iron shape and grinned sheepishly.

"I didn't burn anything else," he said. "Honestly."

"You've been made redundant!" she wailed. "Oh, no, I knew it . . ."

"No . . . no, it's nothing like that," he said quickly. "In fact, I've applied to go on a training course so I'll be eligible for promotion."

She sank on to a chair.

"Do you feel all right, Anthea?"

"I feel a bit . . . dizzy," she confessed. "This isn't real. It doesn't feel real."

She pinched her arm hard and let out a yelp of pain. "I'm not dreaming, anyway."

"Of course you're not dreaming, darling," he said. "Look, are you sure you're comfortable there? Would you like to sit on a cushion or anything?"

"Why should I sit on a cushion?" she cried with a frown.

He gave her tummy a gentle pat, then smiled a knowing smile.

"I've turned over a new leaf. From now on, I'm going to do my share of the chores," he said, and "I'll wash up," he insisted when they'd finished their meal.

She didn't argue, but went meekly off to the lounge.

He found her sitting on the floor with all the baby stuff scattered around her. His heart soared with pride and love.

She looked up at him and smiled before packing it all neatly into the bath, scattering coloured cotton-wool balls around it all.

"What do you think?" she said. "Suzi from the office is off on maternity leave from tomorrow and we all clubbed together and made up a sort of start pack for her."

"It's — it's lovely," he said, swallowing the big lump in his throat.

"Hey, are you all right, Ben?"

Disappointment flooded through his veins like a torrent. He'd planned to be there for the ante-natal classes, in on the birth — everything.

He'd wanted to spoil her — and the baby.

Still, it didn't change the way he felt about her. He still loved her and always would, babies or no babies.

"I'll make some coffee," he said, and kissed the top of her head.

There was no need to turn the leaf back again. As a matter of fact, he'd enjoyed taking care of her and would continue to do so.

"Ben," she called, holding up a soft white romper suit, pressing it against her cheek, "this one isn't for Suzi. This is for us.

"You see, I'm going to have a baby, too." ▪

98

Treasure The Memories

by Della Galton

For so long I'd hoarded them like a miser, but now it was time to cash them in for some real happiness . . .

I WONDER, as I dust blusher across my cheeks, why I'm taking so much trouble. It's been a long time since we last met, another lifetime, I sometimes think.

I can hear your voice in my imagination, *"So much for water under the bridge, Lyndsey."* There'll be a sigh in your voice, a sigh for things past, a shadow in the deep blue of your eyes.

My stomach tightens involuntarily and I think, *madness to go back, madness to even believe it might be possible.*

I twirl before my mirror, glad I'm thinner than I was then. The green jersey dress I've chosen for the occasion shows off the flat planes of my stomach, flattering and feminine.

You loved femininity. You loved the way my hair fell halfway down my back. You liked to twine it around your fingers, pulling me gently towards your waiting lips.

One particular week shines bright in my memory. It was our first holiday, a whole week when we had only ourselves to please.

We stayed in an activity centre in Exmouth, where they offered archery and rock climbing and canoeing, as well as the more usual badminton and swimming.

Neither of us liked sitting around doing nothing, so it was perfect. The weather was perfect, too, as if someone had arranged it specially. The first week of summer saved up for our holiday.

Even the drive down was special. We listened to music and I stretched my hands out of the top of the sun roof, feeling freedom rush past my fingertips.

From time to time I'd glance sideways at you, watching the concentration on your face, admiring the strength and confidence of your hands on the steering-wheel.

I remember thinking, *I'm happy, completely and utterly happy.* All I wanted was to hold on to the feeling, gather it up into my eager arms and keep it close to me, forever and ever.

We abseiled and canoed on the first day, straining most of our muscles and laughing till we ached. On the second day we went riding — or at least I did.

I rode out across the purple-heathered moors, my mind drifting with the rhythm of the horse beneath me.

When I got back you showed me a barn owl you'd discovered perched up in the old stone archway of a disused stable block.

On the third day we felt that we'd done enough to relax a little.

By chance, we found a field, high up on the moors, stone walled and secluded. The yellow grass had been left to its own devices and it danced and rippled like the sea. We sat down amongst it, invisible to the world, and simply lay in each other's arms.

Again it's the freedom I remember. The warmth of sunlight on my hair, the gentle touch of your fingers on my face, your lips on mine. It was a perfect moment, and if dark clouds edged the horizon, then they were tomorrow's clouds. They weren't a part of this wonderful now.

My chiffon and gossamer memories . . .

That week stood out like beacon of hope amongst the darker weeks that would eventually follow it.

I TAKE one last look in my mirror. I've had my hair cut since then. It swirls in a bob around my shoulders. It is a symbol of the new me, the little girl that you loved and left has grown up now.

I wonder if you'll like the woman . . .

Perhaps I should hate you, but I don't, although it hasn't always been so. When you first told me about Anne, I hated you with an intensity that bit deep.

How could you decide you preferred this Anne's company to mine?

I couldn't see anything special about her. The one time that I met her I hurled abuse at her, ignoring the blank dismissiveness in her eyes. I wanted to hurt, to burn and destroy, until there was nothing left but ashes.

It was only afterwards that I realised what a sour taste ashes leave in your mouth. It wasn't her fault that you'd left me and if I was honest, I wasn't blameless either.

When we met, you were coming to terms with the betrayal of your wife and best friend. Now I can see you needed space to sort out your life, to make provision for your son, Jamie, who was just starting out at college and desperately hurt by your divorce.

You didn't need me, clinging and possessive and hinting at being the next Mrs Martell.

You needed space, but I was too full of plans for our wonderful future to understand. I didn't see the signs, didn't notice the increasing tension in your eyes. Selfishly, I'd be upset if a few days went by when you couldn't see me.

By the time I'd learned what you needed, it was, of course, too late.

I've had relationships since then. Two of them, both gone now, both consigned to the bottom drawer of experience.

Perhaps they would have survived. There were actually moments when I thought they were what I wanted, but the bright weeks with you still shone in my memory. It was like sipping cider after champagne.

I heard on the grapevine that you'd finished with Anne. The same people told me that you'd gone out with one or two others. All the time I berated myself for hoping you might ring me. But when you did ring, I was so shocked I was almost breathless. Still, I'd learned by then. I'd learned how to conceal, how to control my emotions.

"A drink? That would be nice. No, Tuesday's out, I'm afraid. Wednesday? Yes, that sounds fine. Yes, I'll meet you there, shall I?"

Madness to go back, I think again. *Madness to even believe it might be possible.*

I step out of my front door on the way to the car and glance at my watch to make sure I'm running just a little bit late.

It's a while before I see you in the dark gloom of the pub. You are sitting in a corner, your hand resting easily on the table, your face still as marble, while mine is tingling with the winter air.

"Hi." I lower my bag over the back of a chair, sit down opposite, and watch the smile spread slowly across the stillness of your face.

In that moment I notice there's more grey in your hair, more lines around your eyes, but you still look beautiful. Serene as you always looked, yet somehow more relaxed.

"Hello, Lyndsey." The chocolate quietness of your voice does nothing to slow the hammering of my heart. "You're looking very well. What would you like to drink?"

"I'll get it."

"No, you won't." The warmth in your voice brushes away my objections as you stand. "What will it be?"

"Oh, the usual," I answer mischievously, wondering if you'll remember, but you don't comment, just stroll across to the bar in that long, easy walk of yours that is so desperately, achingly familiar.

While we talk it is as if we've never been apart — as if the love and the hate drift unremembered across the smoky air.

We are alone again, alone in the lunch-time crowd.

I tell you about my promotion at work and the extension I've just had added to my bungalow.

You talk about your business, the new product you've just designed. As always, your hands are eloquent as you talk, and now and then I get the impression you'd like to touch me.

With sharp longing, I remember those brief butterfly touches that were such an integral part of you.

I'm half dreaming, lost in the familiarity and newness of it all, when you say, "Dorinda, her name's Dorinda. I only met her last week."

Dorinda, the name catches like a knife in my throat.

Am I too late again? Four years and one week too late. But I hear myself saying, "How lovely," and I fix my smile as you talk about her sweet personality and waist-length hair.

I don't want to know about her hair. I don't want to know how nice she is, but all the time I can feel your eyes on me.

You have a way of looking at me that reaches far beyond observation — right into my soul. But this time

I'm better equipped to make sure that you don't see what's there.

Four years of pride encase my emotion and it's the pride that I want you to see.

Later we stand in the car park, your car and mine side by side. You touch me for the first time, taking my hands in yours. A friendship touch, I think bitterly, as I let my hands go light and cool. You won't tell anything from them.

Your eyes are searching my face again and I look back steadily. Then I hear myself saying, "Good luck with Dorinda then", and I'm proud to hear there's not a flicker of a tremble in my voice.

"Thanks." Your voice is uncertain and there's a small frown on your face as if you're somehow puzzled by my words.

"I — I'm sure I'll like her a lot when I get to know her. Jamie's certainly smitten."

"Jamie?" It's my turn for uncertainty. I can feel confusion flooding my face with colour.

"Yes. It really does seem serious this time. I know he's only twenty-two, but she's such a lovely girl. She — she reminds me of you a bit, actually."

My head is light and spinning and without realising I've moved, I find we're standing kissing distance apart, while around us the winter sunlight dances off the tarmac coldness of the car park.

"Would you — would you like to meet up again?" you ask, and I realise my hands are still in yours and that I'm trembling ever so slightly.

"Yes," I say, all pretence at casualness gone, because my heart is dancing alongside the winter sunlight and the car park looks suddenly more beautiful than any summer garden.

"I know I hurt you badly," you continue softly, your eyes still on mine, and I nod slowly and say, "It sometimes takes two."

I'm suddenly aware that we're still holding hands, that your touch is warm and very reassuring and that perhaps I should pull away.

For a moment I have a feeling that you know exactly what I'm thinking, but you just remark idly, "Your hair suits you like that."

I grin at you. Memories are flooding back of the way we used to be. How we could talk for hours without saying anything important at all, and how a few short sentences could express much more than the words themselves.

I have to let go of your hands eventually because I can't open my car door until I do, but I can see you smiling in my rear-view mirror as I drive out of the car park.

Once more I think about yesterday's chiffon and gossamer memories, but this time recognise their fragility.

Today's, tomorrow's, memories will be stronger, more solid, with many facets — just like a handful of diamonds . . . ■

A Man's Best Friend

by Teresa Ashby

From now on, it was supposed to be just his beloved dog and him. But it seemed his kindly house-cleaner had other ideas!

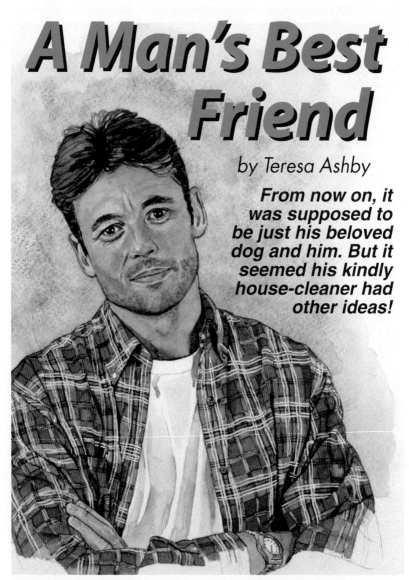

W ELL, Kelly," Paul said, hands on hips as he surveyed the chaos before him, "this is it — home sweet home. What do you think?"

Kelly didn't think anything. He was far too busy sniffing frantically around an overflowing tea chest, wondering where his food bowl had vanished to.

The St Bernard turned and wagged his tail, giving Paul a look which was far too intelligent for a mere canine. He found it quite spooky at times just how much that hound understood.

"I know I put the tin opener in one of these chests," Paul said.

Of course, Barbara would have known exactly where to lay her hands on it.

She would have labelled all the boxes and chests and he wouldn't be in the position he was now, with boxes of bed-linen and towels piled up in the living-room and all his kitchen equipment upstairs in the main bedroom.

"I'll take a look upstairs," he said. "It's got to turn up sooner or later."

He was halfway up when the doorbell rang and Kelly bounced into the tiny hall, barking ferociously and wagging his tail like mad.

Paul ordered Kelly to his bed and opened the door to find himself looking down at a tiny woman wearing a neat, stone-coloured anorak and a colourful headscarf.

"Ivy Bayliss!" she said.

"Er, sorry — not with you," Paul replied, puzzled.

Kelly wafted by in search of his bed, which hadn't yet been unpacked.

Ivy Bayliss narrowed her eyes and looked up at Paul. "'Twas you put card in newsagent's window, wunnit?"

"Oh, for a cleaning lady? Yes."

"Well, I don't do outside winders, but I'll put me hand to most other things . . . though I dunno 'bout that dog."

She peered past him and gave Kelly a wary look. Paul looked at Kelly — he who wouldn't say woof to a cat.

Ivy clasped her chin in her hand. "Still, you look like you'll do. When can I start?"

"Are you any good at making tea?"

She grinned at him. "Any good at it? If it was an Olympic sport, I'd win gold every time!"

"Then come in, Mrs Bayliss, and I'll see if I can find the kettle and you can start right away!"

Kelly liked Ivy Bayliss. He sat next to her with his great big head resting on her knee while she tickled his ears.

"He misses my wife — my ex-wife," Paul said sadly. "He was her dog really, but when she left me, she left him, too."

"Ah, he's a lady's dog, is he? So, she left you, did she?" Ivy said. "Why was that then?"

BEFORE he knew it, he'd reeled off his life story while Ivy listened. "You need looking after, Mr Hunter," she said. "Some people aren't cut out to live alone — and you're one of them."

"I have Kelly . . ."

She looked doubtful, then asked, "Do you want me to call round every day?"

"Every day, Monday to Friday," he confirmed. "Just to keep the place neat and clean, and walk the dog."

She looked down at the big head resting on her lap.

"Cooking?"

"I beg your pardon?"

"If you're going to communicate every day, you won't have a lot of time to eat."

"Communicate?" He frowned. "Oh, commute. I see."

"I can do you a casserole or a pie. I do a lovely steak and kidney pud — ask anyone."

"Well, yes, thank you. Thank you very much indeed, Mrs B, that would be just great."

"Will you be getting one of them stattey-lights? I do like to watch a bit of telly when I have my morning cuppa and I've noticed in the paper they have some good films on the stattey-light."

"I wasn't planning to," he admitted, but she looked so crestfallen and disappointed he heard himself add hastily, "but I'll probably consider it."

She brightened up at that.

"Now, then," she went on, "what about money? I'll want extra for walking your St Bruno."

When he told her what he used to pay his cleaning lady in London, she gasped.

"Is that not enough?" he asked nervously.

"It'll do," she said. "I'll start Monday then."

BY the weekend, Paul had decided that he was going to enjoy village life very much indeed.

He'd always wanted to live in the country, but it was something that Barbara hated.

"All those spiders and bats and rodents — ugh!" she'd shuddered.

But Paul enjoyed watching the bats swoop around the eaves at dusk, or waking up to find his lawn full of rabbits basking in the early-morning sunshine.

His first Monday back at work came as quite a wrench.

The noise and dirt of the city seemed to jar more than usual and a dark cloud settled over him until it was time to go home.

Kelly was ecstatic to see him. He bounded around the tiny cottage like an hysterical Baloo, all shaggy coat and smiley-faced.

"Did you miss me?" Paul asked, but, of course, he already knew the answer.

Ivy Bayliss had left him a Cornish pasty the size of a dinner plate and a very interesting-looking salad.

He took it outside so that he could watch the sun go down as he ate.

"Isn't this marvellous, Kelly?" he said to the dog. "Paradise."

"I don't know about that," a voice said, making him jump. "You've really upset the apple cart now, I can tell you!"

He spun round and found himself looking at a rather formidable-looking woman in jodhpurs and an over-tight hacking jacket.

"Me?" Paul glared accusingly at Kelly. "What have you done now?" he hissed.

"The dog's done nothing!" the woman trumpeted. "It's to do with that exasperating woman Ivy Bayliss, of course."

"Mrs B?"

"Mrs B, indeed! Now, perhaps Mrs Hunter is here?"

"Mrs Hunter isn't here."

"Very well." She sniffed. "It won't do, Mr Hunter, it won't do at all. You're not living in the city now and what you can get away with there, you certainly won't get away with around here!"

"I don't know what you're talking about," he said.

What on earth had Ivy been saying? He racked his brain trying to remember exactly what he'd said when he'd rattled off his life story.

"That's the trouble with you being a man," this strange woman went on. "I'll have to come back when your wife's at home."

She didn't give him the chance to tell her his wife wasn't going to be home, before she stomped off back the way she'd come.

THE next evening he returned home to a clean house, a tired dog and a trout which merely had to be put in the oven for a few minutes along with some duchesse potatoes.

"You're a treasure, Mrs B," he said to the air.

Afterwards, he was about to leave with Kelly for a twilight stroll, when two ladies, so alike they had to be sisters, appeared in his front garden.

They made a huge fuss of Kelly, then turned and glared at him with twin expressions of outrage.

"What did I do this time?" he asked.

"You really should stress upon Ivy Bayliss the importance of discretion. She's caused no end of trouble with that loose tongue of hers."

Paul rubbed his chin, puzzled.

"Perhaps we could talk with Mrs Hunter?" one of the ladies suggested, trying to see past him into the cottage.

It sounded like the third degree to Paul as he said politely, "Look, I'm sorry. I have to dash." With an apologetic smile, he and Kelly hurried on their way.

The following day, he came home from work rather less happily than the day before, carrying a battered cardboard box.

Mr Matthews, his boss, had called him into the office and handed him a white envelope.

He'd clutched the envelope and heard one or two words such as "cutbacks", "over-staffed" and "profit-margins" and lots of other words with hyphens in between, that spelled the end of his career.

Then Mr Matthews suggested he visit the supermarket next door and get a box so that he could clear his desk.

Well, at least he didn't have a mortgage to worry about now. He'd bought the cottage outright.

Still, he had other bills to pay and one rather large mouth to feed.

And, of course, there was Mrs B. How was she going to take to being laid off just a few days into her new job?

He told Kelly what had happened.

"It will mean that I'll be able to spend more time with you, of course," he added, and Kelly looked pleased about that.

★★★★

He'd taken his meal, a spectacular-looking quiche with a huge bowl of salad and two large baked potatoes, into the garden.

"Egg and chips for me from now on," he said wistfully to Kelly. "But, oh dear, what on earth am I going to do about Mrs B?"

"That's easy! Tell her to behave!"

He whirled round and saw a young woman in a pretty floral dress standing on the lawn.

Kelly raced up to greet her and she made a fuss of him as if she'd known him all his life.

"Your 'St Bruno' and I have already met," she said with a wry smile. "Actually, he has a daily romp round the meadow with Cedric — my Columbus."

"Columbus?"

"My clumber spaniel."

"What can I do for you, Mrs . . . er?"

"It's Miss," she said, smiling. "Carla Holland."

"Would you like to sit down?"

She sat on the bench and he felt oddly unsettled by her presence. Pretty girls did not fit into his scheme of things.

"Mrs B can sniff out a refugee from the city at least a mile away," Carla said. "I bet she was knocking on your door before you'd even started your unpacking."

"As a matter of fact," he said uneasily, "she was."

"I thought so. She's a crafty one, our Ivy."

"So . . . does she work for you, too, then?" Paul said.

"You could say that. I run the craft shop from the Black Barn on Blackthorn Lane. "Ivy provides me with home-made conserves and some pretty potent strawberry and rhubarb wine."

"I've seen the shop," he said. "You do corn dollies and those dried flower arrangements."

"Among other things," she said. "Anyway, I just thought I should warn you that quite a few noses have been put out of joint since your arrival!

"Perhaps if I talked to your wife . . ."

"Oh, I see. You're another one, aren't you? Coming here, fishing for information! Well, I'll tell you, there is no Mrs Hunter. She's Mrs Vincent now and no, I don't have any children, either, just Kelly here.

"I take a size ten shoe and I don't like cabbage, but I am partial to chocolate mousse. Is there anything else you'd like to know?"

CARLA stared at him in complete and utter amazement. He'd amazed himself — he had no idea he could be so rude and arrogant.

"I'm sorry . . ." he began, but she was on her feet, her face flushed.

"I only came to help," she said.

"Please, sit down. It's just...I know it's no excuse for being unpleasant, but I was made redundant today and I'm not in the best of moods."

She sank down, her face taking on an expression of genuine sympathy.

"Oh, I'm so sorry. I know just how that feels. It happened to me, too, but in my case it was the best thing that could have happened.

"I came here, started my own little business and earn enough to live comfortably on."

He grinned. "Well, if you're in the market for carved wooden animals, I do a mean duck!" he said, not really seriously.

But Carla's face lit up.

"Hand-carved wooden animals? Do you know, I'm constantly being asked by visitors for that sort of thing. I can get them from outside, but I prefer to sell locally-produced stock."

"Hear that, Kelly?" Paul said. "You might not have to starve after all! My wooden salad servers could save us yet!"

"Oh, it won't come to that," Carla said cheerfully. "Mrs B says you're an accountant. You could work from home for yourself."

She made it sound so easy.

"I could use some help with my books, so you could consider me your first customer!"

It sounded promising, but something was still worrying Paul.

"Exactly what have I done to upset everyone?" he asked.

She gave him a warm smile. "Don't worry, I made exactly the same mistake when I moved here two years ago."

"What mistake?"

"Mrs B's hourly rate, of course. You're paying her London rates, which are way above what the locals pay."

"So that's the problem! All the cleaning ladies are up in arms because their employers are too mean to pay them the going rate — and I get the blame!"

"You've got a lot to learn," Carla said. "It doesn't cost as much to live here as it does in London. Still, I'm sure you'll think of a way round it. The only thing I don't understand is why she let you make the same mistake, knowing the trouble I got into!"

IVY BAYLISS arrived the following morning with two bulging shopping bags.

She was humming to herself as she let herself into the kitchen and didn't see Paul sitting there.

"Hello, Kelly, you lovely St Bernard!" she said, giving the dog a huge hug. "I'll warm you up a bit of milk, then we'll go out for a nice walk. We might even see Carla and her little clumber spaniel!"

Paul cleared his throat and she spun round.

"Oh, it's you! I thought it was burgey-lars! Why aren't you off then, communicating?"

He shook his head. "It's no use, Mrs B," he said. "I heard you talking to Kelly just now."

She shrugged her shoulders and sat down. "Oh, well."

"Why do you do it?"

"People expect you to be a bit eccentric," she explained. "They like me messing my words up. Makes them feel superior."

"Superior — to you?" Paul guffawed. "That'll be the day!"

"What are you doing here?" she asked. "Day off, is it?"

Briefly, he explained his new circumstances.

"Oh, well, that's the way things are these days," Ivy said. "I suppose that means you won't be wanting me around any more."

"On the contrary," he said. "I'll be putting the cottage on the market and moving back to the city. But, until it's sold, I'll need someone to keep the place looking nice for prospective buyers."

"Of course," she said briskly. "But I won't be paid London rates if you're not earning a London salary. You can pay me the local rate.

"So you've met Carla?" she added.

Her eyes narrowed as she watched carefully for his response.

He had to try not to smile too broadly. Oh, yes, he'd met Carla — and she'd made quite an impression!

"I don't gossip about my ladies and gentlemen, Mr Hunter, you should know that," Mrs B's eyes began to twinkle and she gave him a mischievous little smile. "But she walks her spaniel on the common every morning about this time."

He reached for Kelly's lead.

"Take your time," Mrs B said, "and I'll make some nice open sandwiches for lunch with prawns and salad."

"That'd be great, thanks!"

I'll make enough sandwiches for two — but I won't be staying," she said meaningfully.

"That's very sweet of you, Mrs B, but I'm not sure I'll be able to work up such an appetite."

She gritted her teeth, grimaced and shook her head.

"I'll make enough for two," she repeated, "just in case you want to bring anyone home for lunch!"

Finally catching her drift, he gave in to an impulse and gave Mrs B a hug, then he hurried off towards the common where he could see Carla .

She looked even lovelier than she had last night and, when she saw him and smiled and waved, he felt as if he'd known her forever.

Cedric and Kelly bowled off together as Carla fell into step beside him and Paul suddenly understood why Ivy Bayliss had let him make the mistake of paying her too much money.

It wasn't because she was greedy or because she wanted to stir up trouble, but because she knew Carla would try to rescue him!

"Hi," he said softly.

"Hi," she murmured.

"I know this might sound strange but, do you like open sandwiches with prawns?"

"My favourite!" she exclaimed. "Ivy always makes them for me as a special treat. Why?"

He threw back his head and laughed.

Carla was right, Ivy Bayliss was a crafty one — but her heart was in the right place.

In a little while, he'd ask Carla back for lunch, but first he'd help her gather some material and maybe look for some wood so he could get started.

Then they could talk about her accounts and he could cancel that appointment he'd made with the estate agent.

You had to start somewhere — and he just couldn't think of any place better than right here. ■

Full Circle

by Della Galton

Remembering the contentment of her childhood rekindled a flame of hope for the future.

T is almost impossible not to slam the door. I want to slam it, want to slam away some of the anger and frustration, but it wouldn't be fair. I keep telling myself that it isn't her fault, but it's hard to believe because she looks the same. She still has the same white hair and her eyes are still the same summer blue. Yet here there is a difference.

Where once there was a sharp intelligence, there's now a vague emptiness.

Yesterday she came across me in the kitchen while I was chopping up carrots for dinner. Bewildered, she stood in the doorway, staring at me. "Who are you . . .? What are you doing here?" she'd asked.

"I'm making dinner for us, Mother."

"But how did you get in? Did I leave the door unlocked?" And she wandered over to the back door, removed the key and put it in her house-coat pocket.

It was at times like these that I wanted to shout, "Mum, it's me!" For a moment I was even tempted to take her by the shoulders and shake the fuzziness from her brain. Instead I kept my voice quiet and calm.

"A nice dinner. That's what I'm making. Would you like that? Are you hungry?"

But by then she'd lost interest and was sitting at the kitchen table, stirring a cup of cold coffee, turning the spoon round and round so that it scraped the sides of the cup, until eventually I had to take it away from her.

TODAY it's Sunday, the day Jilly Henderson, the district nurse, drops by to see how we're getting on. She's a kind, pleasant soul.

She took one look at my face and said, "Why don't you go out for a walk, dear?"

You see, today isn't an ordinary Sunday. Today Jilly is going to ask me how much longer I think I can cope with looking after my mother single-handed, and I really don't know how I'm going to reply.

Aware of Jilly's anxious eyes on me, I'd managed to force some false calmness into my voice and I'd said, "Thanks, a walk would be nice," but I'd really wanted to say, *If I go out, I might not come back.*

I might not come back because I can't stand another day of this nightmare. Everything my mother used to be is gone, and only this stranger with my mother's face remains.

Alzheimer's.

Until last August it had just been another word, a medical word, another illness. Something that happened to other people.

I can feel myself frowning and so I try to relax away some of the tension. For half an hour or so I'm free and it's nice to feel early summer sun on my face.

As I pass No.40, ten-year-old Thomas comes out of the front gate with a puppy on a lead that is far too long to be of much use.

"Hello, Miss Laing, what do you think of my new puppy?"

I force brightness into my voice, "Very nice, Tom. Very nice."

"He's called Nipper," he says, and the puppy bounces up and down at the sound of his name.

"Nipper — sit!" and Nipper jumps up joyfully so that Tom overbalances and ends up sitting on the pavement.

"He gets too excited. He's better in the park, much better. He's as good as gold in the park."

"I'm sure he is," I say, and stupidly I want to cry.

Perhaps it's because Nipper and Tom remind me of my own childhood.

I haven't dared to think about the past lately. I haven't dared to think about the mother who kissed things better, the mother who scolded and sighed when I accidentally knocked her Wedgwood teapot off the shelf and not so accidentally hid the pieces in the bin.

I remember how guilty I felt then, but it's nothing to the guilt I feel now.

I think about the conversation I had with Jilly Henderson last week.

"You mustn't blame yourself and you mustn't feel guilty. I know how distressing it can be, but you can't carry on by yourself forever, dear. No-one can, believe me."

Her voice was warm and professional and I desperately wanted to believe her, but we were talking about doing something I'd always sworn I'd never do.

We were talking about putting my mother in a home.

TOM and Nipper are dancing ahead of me and I follow them in the direction of the park, because I can't go back. I can't go back crying, and as I walk, the memories creep painfully and uninvited into my mind.

It was a bright, blustery day in May just like today.

It was the day I found a tiny brown and white scrap of a terrier in the woods at the back of our house and I took him home to Mum, hoping fervently that she'd say we could keep him.

"He must have an owner somewhere," she said, but although we advertised in the pet shop and the post office, no owner materialised.

Toby was my dog from the beginning. I loved him with that fierce burning love that you can feel for a dog, but that you can't feel for your parents when you're young. They're just there, fussing and caring and taken for granted, whereas Toby was my ally and my best friend.

He slept on my bed, or sometimes even *in* it so that Mum wouldn't see him when she'd come in to say goodnight.

At least that's what I thought at the time. Years later she told me of the times she had to bite her lip in order not to laugh when she saw Toby wiggling uncooperatively beneath the blankets.

I even took him to school once, tucked into my satchel with his nose poking out the top. We were having a "wildlife" day and had been asked to bring in examples.

Miss Marston took me to one side, however, and quietly explained that actually she'd meant us to bring in fallen twigs and acorns and things like that.

★★★★

At the park Tom lets the puppy off the lead and I watch them run across the springy grass.

There's a part of me that still longs for their innocence . . .

When I was ten, Toby was hit by a car when we were out walking. He'd run across the road, chasing a squirrel, and the car hadn't been able to stop.

The man driving it was almost as upset as I was. He let me sit in the back with Toby whimpering on my knee while he drove us to the vet's.

"Don't worry, he'll be OK," the vet said, as he bent to take the little dog from my arms.

Later that afternoon, I stood in the hallway while Mother phoned from the kitchen to see how Toby was.

She was talking too quietly for me to hear everything she said, but I thought I heard her say, "Yes, I'd agree. It would probably be for the best . . ."

When she replaced the receiver her face was serious.

"What did the vet say? Did he say Toby can come home soon?"

"I'm afraid Toby won't be coming back, darling," she said gently. "You see he's gone to heaven . . . He's gone to the little dogs' heaven in the sky."

I felt something snap inside me and I wrenched my hand away from hers. "He hasn't gone to heaven. He's coming back to live with us. He is! I *know* he is."

It took a week of hardly eating and hardly sleeping, and a week of my mother's unstinting patience before I would believe that Toby wasn't coming back. The Tuesday after the accident she sat down beside me on the sofa.

"Darling, I would give anything for this not to have happened, but it has happened and I can't bear to see you like this."

I didn't look at her because tears were coming again but she pulled me into her arms anyway.

She carried on speaking gently. "Sometimes life changes in ways we don't want it to, in ways that hurt us. But there's nothing we can do about it.

"The hurt will get better, I promise you. It will take time, but it will get better."

I didn't answer. It was the beginning of the school holidays and already I was mourning all the unwalked walks, the unplayed games with my beloved dog.

She was right, of course. Eventually the rawness of the pain did begin to ease, but I'd lost something important and precious, something that was more than my little dog's presence.

It was several years later that I realised that perhaps a part of me had been mourning for the passing of my childhood.

It was also several years later that I found out that Toby hadn't died of his injuries as I'd believed. His back legs had been crushed so badly that the vet had told my mother that his only hope was to remove them.

Mother had decided that it would be kinder in the long run if Toby was put to sleep.

It can't have been an easy decision to make, but she'd made it because she'd thought it was the right thing to do. She'd thought it was for the best.

There's an ache in my heart as I think she'll never be able to make another decision. It's up to me now. It's up to me to do what I think is best, because somehow Mother and I have come full circle.

IT'S getting chilly now. The sun has gone. I've been sitting still too long, thinking too long.

From across the park Tom waves at me. "See you then, Miss Laing," and I glance at my watch and realise that I, too, should be getting back.

Jilly will want to leave soon. There won't be time for us to talk now. There won't be time to sit and discuss my lost mother's future.

A few minutes later I let myself into the house. Jilly meets me at the door and I ask, "How has she been?"

"Oh, she's been fine." Jilly smiles, her eyes scanning my face. "How about you? You look better for your walk."

"Thanks. I feel better." I hang my coat up on the stand in the hallway. "Is it all right if we talk next week?"

"Of course it is, dear. And you know where I am in the meantime if you need me."

"Thanks," I say again and this time I manage to return her smile. She says her goodbyes and I wait while she fetches her bike.

She pedals away, not looking back, and I watch her for a while before shutting the front door on the outside world. Then I go into the lounge where Mother sits in front of the television.

She doesn't look at me. She's laughing at something on the screen and as I watch her I'm inundated with memories.

I can feel them rushing through me, a kaleidoscope of memories. Years of them that cannot possibly be wiped out because of this illness over which my mother has no control.

I go across to her and bend and kiss the top of her head and she twists round and smiles at me. She probably doesn't know who I am, but for once I think, does it matter? Does it really matter as long as she can smile?

"I love you, Mum," I say in a fierce whisper and she nods vaguely and turns back to the television and I think, we'll cope, you and I — for a time, anyway.

Some day soon the changes will have to be made and I'll have to be brave enough to make them.

But for now, it's enough that we're together . . . ∎

Kate's Priceless Lesson

by Carol Wood

It took an old dog-eared slip of paper to show her how much she had been missing . . .

F I hear just once more about somebody suing someone else, I'm going to scream — and very loudly!" Kate screwed up her eyes and ran slim, ringless fingers through her hair.

Conflicts, rows over who keeps what and who lives where! Wasn't there anyone who lived happily ever after these days?

It must be a bad day, Kate scolded herself later, as she walked through the shopping centre at quarter past one.

Or perhaps six years with the same law firm was finally turning her into a cynic!

Not to mention the painful memories of Nick . . .

She forced her mind away from Nick Brompton, thinking that at least she had learned one thing since their break-up — to stand on her own two feet and make her own little nest.

Kate soon found herself in a side street she knew well, staring into Mr Howard's antique shop window.

And there she saw it . . . It was beautiful — just what she wanted!

She'd bought quite a few of the things for the flat here, and there was always a warm welcome, sometimes even a cup of tea if there wasn't another customer.

"Need any help?"

Kate jumped as a dark head appeared from behind a pine wardrobe. A pair of eyes, the colour of burnished conkers, surveyed her with interest.

"I . . . er . . . was looking at that desk, the one over there. I suppose it's expensive, is it?"

"Haven't a clue, actually." The brown eyes were set into a smiling face under a shock of chestnut hair. "My grandfather should have left a price on it. Help yourself!"

Kate nodded. It was a bit off-putting not having Mr Howard to chat to.

The only sticker on the desk recorded a price which, luckily, wasn't above her limit. "Around the thirties . . . forties period, is it?" Kate enquired. She knew a fair bit about antiques now.

Since Nick, she'd made sure she'd stuck to realities, things she could touch and be certain of. Things which wouldn't just disappear . . .

"Search me. All I can tell you is it hasn't got any woodworm.

"I persuaded my grandfather to have a few weeks off while I fill in. I haven't a clue about antiques. Plants, now, they're more my line."

"Well . . . this desk's not an antique, but it's what your grandfather might call a collectable," Kate told him. "Would it be possible for you to deliver, do you think?"

"How about the day after tomorrow, when I've closed the shop?"

"Fine!"

Kate paid for the desk, gave her address and happily hurried back to work.

There was something wonderful about spending hard-earned money on something you really liked. But today, the feeling didn't last long.

Every time the phone rang, someone yelled at her. Why couldn't the world just stop yelling at itself?

When she said as much to Jane, her friend laughed.

"Heavens, Kate! Don't you realise you're missing all the fun? Life is painful sometimes, sure, but it's wonderful, too. You don't know what you're missing by isolating yourself since . . . Oh, Kate, I'm sorry! I don't mean to harp on about Nick, but it's been almost two years!"

Jane meant well, Kate realised, but it still hurt.

SHE'D met Nick at college and fallen madly, deeply, in love. Not that he hadn't warned her that he didn't want to settle down.
He told her it was a career in photography he wanted, not marriage.

But she'd always hoped, right up until that assignment in London — and Tricia. Tricia was so beautiful — enough to turn any man's head.

★★★★

On Friday evening, Kate hurried home from work, cleared a space in the alcove and opened the door to Mr Howard's grandson, who hauled in the desk with the help of another man.

It only just fitted, its high ornate back and umpteen drawers all rather cumbersome.

The young man glanced around the room. "My goodness, what a lot you've packed in here!"

Not a very flattering way to describe her lovely possessions, Kate thought, rather put out. But, as they'd lugged the desk up two flights of stairs, she offered them a cup of tea.

"Brilliant!" Mr Howard's grandson exclaimed. But the other man excused himself and hurried off to the pub for a "proper drink."

Kate prepared the tea and set it out on her Victorian table overlaid with her white linen and lace tablecloth.

"Crikey!" Adam Howard — she'd now learned his name — frowned at the array of dainty, Minton bone china and the delicate cake stand.

"Do I actually drink and eat from these?" Then, grinning hungrily, he pounced on a macaroon and ingeniously threaded his large brown fingers through the handle of his teacup.

He and Ben, the other deskmover, owned a garden centre outside of town, she was told in between mouthfuls.

He noticed Kate had no plants.

"Nothing growing!" he observed, astonished. "I'll bring you something to liven up the desk."

The following Monday, he brought her a willowy green fern, but she was afraid it would need a lot of attention. "I really couldn't accept it!" she protested.

"Rubbish! All it needs is a couple of ice cubes from the fridge each day. Simple!" And so the fern was installed.

Then he brought a basket flooded with flowers and trailing ivy.

"I'll never keep them. They'll die! I'm hopeless with living things, Adam."

"Then I'll show you how to be good. You'll see green shoots and new growth, you'll get hooked on it — and you won't have to worry because I'll check them regularly for you.

"At no cost, mind, just a cup of tea . . ."

She didn't want him to check, or to come around. Who did he think he was, turning the flat into a . . . a florist's!

Politely, she told him so and he didn't show up again.

She frantically watered the plants, even talked to them, checking every leaf, knowing with a terrible certainty she didn't have green fingers. They would die and she would be left all the emptier for once having had the pleasure of them.

And to her horror, the fern went brown at the edges of its lovely soft fronds.

It was on a Saturday morning she noticed and her heart turned over in dismay.

And then there was a knock at the door and she opened it — and Adam Howard peeped out over a long wooden shape wedged in his arms. "I thought you might like a window box . . ." he said, grinning.

"The fern's dying," she blurted out. "Adam, I just don't want the responsibility of anything more!"

"No, it's not." He peered over her shoulder into the flat. "You've over-watered it a bit, but it's not too late. Look, let's get it into the sun . . ."

HE'S gorgeous! Where did you meet him, you snake! How long have you two been . . . ?"

Kate cringed, regretting the day Jane had unexpectedly called into the flat and found Adam inspecting the leaves of a jaded aspidistra.

Over the three months she had known him, his words had been proved prophetic and she was well and truly addicted.

Last night, when he had brought her back from the nursery where she had been helping out, he'd very gently leaned forward at her door to kiss her goodnight.

Panic had flooded through her like a storm tide and she almost jumped into the flat. It was too soon, too quick!

She'd left him with those brown eyes of his just staring at her . . .

And at nights, she would stare around the flat and try not to look at the plants which reminded her. She told herself repeatedly that she'd been sensible.

It was to ease the little pain beneath her ribs that she began resolutely to tidy her life back into neat, secure compartments, starting with the desk she'd bought from the antique shop.

Bills to be paid here, correspondence there, old letters and postcards in another pile on the floor . . . and then, her fingers found a tiny button which, when pressed, flipped open a slim, hidden drawer.

Inside was a book. When she prised open the first page, she realised a diary lay in her hands.

Two hours later, Kate read over one page in particular, again and again.

Last night, we could hear them coming from a long way off. It was like the droning of bees. The fireman dug us out from the Anderson shelter in the morning and there was nothing left of all the things Billy and me owned.

Just the table in the front room and Billy's desk were left. The bomb blew the front door in to meet the back one in the middle of the house! And then everything collapsed.

Kate read on, her heart pounding as though she could actually hear the planes overhead. There was a simple, uncluttered entry, the last, written two weeks later.

The telegram came to Mum's today. Billy is missing in action. The house and the furniture seemed to matter so much once, but nothing matters any more.

Kate closed the diary thoughtfully. The wartime bride had lost a home and a husband and, no doubt, the desk had only served to remind her of her loss.

For, tucked between the back page and the cover, was a browning, faded auction slip dated a year after Billy's death.

KATE deliberately passed by Mr Howard's shop every chance she got for the next few weeks, calling in, eventually, to buy a sewing-chair she had seen in the window.

"It's not very old," Mr Howard told her, running a gnarled, varnish-stained hand through his grey hair. "Not very valuable, Kate."

She searched over his shoulder to where she'd first seen Adam, but the space was vacant, not even the pine wardrobe was there.

"How is Adam?" she asked, finally plucking up courage and feeling her face flush to her hairline.

"Oh . . . fine . . . just fine!" Mr Howard frowned at her thoughtfully. "Look . . . shall I drop the chair in on my way home? You won't want to take it back to the office, will you?"

Kate managed a smile in spite of the disappointment she felt at not hearing a single syllable about Adam.

And, somehow, the act of buying something to make her feel better hadn't worked this time, compounding her gloom.

"About six-ish then?"

And, at precisely five minutes to six, the front doorbell chimed and Kate hurried to the door, not even having had time to take off her coat.

She stood very still, her eyes as round as moons as she opened the door. "Adam . . . !"

Her visitor shifted from one large foot to another and pushed the little chair in front of him. "I've just come to deliver this, Kate.

"I'm doing most of my grandfather's deliveries, you see, and —"

"Come in . . . please!" Kate interrupted, opening the door wide, her heart jumping around like a frog.

"Here do? Or here?" Adam tried the chair in several places while she watched and finally nodded, smiling, as he tucked it by the desk.

Then he moved slowly to the door, reluctant to go. "The fern looks great — and the window box — and the aspidistra . . ."

Kate thought of the diary and hurried to the desk.

"Adam, would you give this to your grandfather? It was in a drawer in the desk. It's not really mine to keep."

As she gave it to him, she looked into the deep brown, puzzled eyes now watching her.

How could she tell him, in a few inadequate words, how much she had learned since she last saw him?

How could she tell him she was prepared to take the risk of loving even if it meant losing?

Kate was to ask herself a thousand times afterwards if it was she who launched herself into Adam's arms, or he who scooped her into his.

"Oh, Katie, I've missed you so much." He held her very close, so close she could hardly breathe. "I've thought of every excuse to come here . . ."

"And I've thought of every excuse to walk past your grandfather's shop just in case I caught a glimpse of you!"

Adam tipped up her chin towards him. "You didn't really want the chair?" he asked her wonderingly.

She found herself smiling then — and the smile transported her into a kind of heaven as he kissed her.

And she knew that, one day, she would tell him everything . . . when their lives were overflowing with the truly priceless treasure of love. ◼

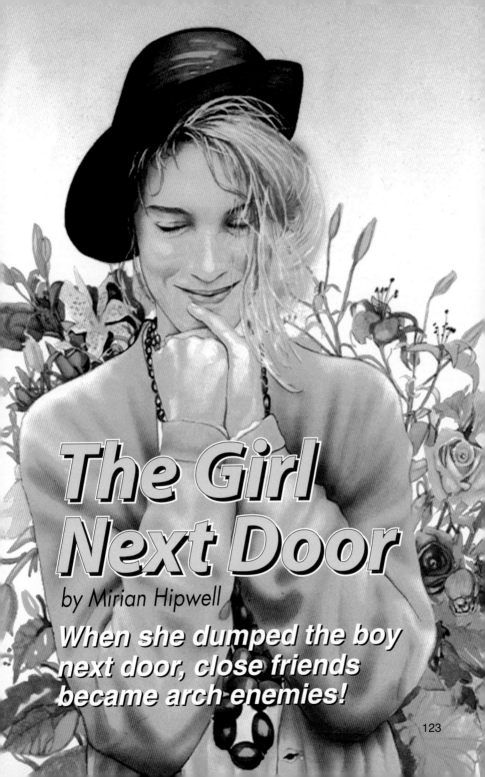

The Girl Next Door

by Mirian Hipwell

When she dumped the boy next door, close friends became arch enemies!

THE driver from Wilson's Building Materials Ltd had managed to lose himself twice already before finding Leyland Square, where he had to drop off a load of sand and bricks. If he hadn't been in such a hurry to get back to the depot for his afternoon tea, he might have taken more care where he deposited the load. Even so, it wouldn't have been easy, number three being squeezed into a corner with very little frontage.

As it was, he was well down the motorway when Janet Baxter arrived home later than she'd expected and found that the load of sand her husband Jim had ordered had been dropped midway between their gate and that of number two.

Even then, it wouldn't have been a major problem. But what Wilson's driver couldn't know was that he had unwittingly dipped his toe into the murky waters of what Janet liked to term, "a difference of opinion".

Inadvertently, he'd caused a ripple which would reverberate into a full blown tidal wave before the week was out.

It was all to do with the Grahams' son, Alex, a bank trainee, and the Baxters' daughter, Elaine, an art student.

Everybody had thought how well they looked together, the pretty girl and the handsome lad. Both families looked on fondly, envisaging a closer relationship.

Ted Graham and Jim Baxter were in the same darts team at the Rose and Crown, and Sheila Graham and Janet Baxter were never out of each other's houses. As for the two youngest, Danny and Mandy, they were inseparable.

All that changed the day Alex came home white-faced and scowling, to shut himself in his bedroom for three hours. It was noticed that Elaine came home alone some time later, and in a mood which warned everyone to steer clear.

There's been a quarrel, both sets of parents thought, shaking their heads wryly and harking back to their own teenage years. It'll all blow over soon enough.

But it wasn't to be that simple. It transpired, when Alex felt able to talk about it, that Elaine had dumped him for a fellow student at the art college.

Despite being upset herself, Sheila probably wouldn't have said anything if it hadn't been for hearing Janet and Elaine laughing together in the garden the following day as she hung out her washing.

Laughing, she'd seethed . . . probably at the expense of her poor son.

She'd gone to the fence and called Janet over.

"I just thought you ought to know that I think your Elaine's behaved very badly."

"Oh? Well, I think she's perfectly entitled to choose who she goes out with."

One thing led to another after that and the exchange of words ended with both women marching into their respective houses, vowing never to speak to each other again.

Ted Graham hadn't meant to get involved at all. But as the days went on, with his wife making herself more and more upset, he felt obliged to have a word over the fence himself.

"Sheila's working herself up into a right state over this," he complained to Jim. "Janet had no call to say what she did. I mean, it's got nothing to do with any of us. It's between the young ones."

"Oh?" Normally a placid man, Ted felt bound to spring to his wife's defence. "Well, that's certainly not the way I heard it."

The quarrel was short and sharp and resulted in Ted Graham finding a new local. This, of course, meant that he would not be available for the darts team, which, frankly, needed every bit of help it could get that year if it was to avoid being relegated.

Even the children got involved.

"I'm not playing with you any more!" Mandy Graham declared when Danny Baxter called round for her.

"I don't care," Danny retorted. "I never liked playing with girls anyway."

The days stretched into weeks, with no sign of a softening on either side. Indeed, when Elaine Baxter brought her new boyfriend home with great ceremony one Sunday afternoon, things turned several shades cooler.

And as the coolness continued, Jim Baxter decided he would build a wall in the back garden where the fence had been so that there'd be no reason for any of them to so much as look at each other again.

This was the state of affairs that prevailed when the lorry from Wilsons dropped its load of sand and bricks several feet to the right of where it should have been dropped.

Ted Graham parked his car as best he could that evening and glowered at the mess by his front kerb.

"Well, I hope he gets that lot cleared up fast," he commented to his wife.

Normally, it would have been no problem. He would have been out there with his spade helping Ted to move it.

But in the present circumstances, all he was prepared to do was fume to himself about the inconvenience of not being able to park on his own drive — and wait. Not for too long either, he thought grimly.

Around six-thirty, Jim Baxter came out of his house, walked to the top of his drive and began to shovel determinedly. Even so, he only managed to move the part of the mound which was obstructing the Grahams' driveway.

Then, with a that's-it-for-tonight-and-you-can-like-it-or-lump-it look over at his neighbour's, he went into his own house.

THE following day, it rained hard. The sand turned heavy and clay-like and everyone brought it into the house on their shoes.

Janet Baxter grew more harassed and her son, Danny, more gleeful.

He was out there the moment the rain cleared up, running up and down the sandy mound, making mud pies and generally having the best time he'd had since his last trip to the seaside.

Mandy Graham watched enviously through the window. At last, unable to stand it any longer, she hurried outside.

"Get lost! You're not playing here," Danny said. "This is our sand."

"He won't let me play in the sand!" she wailed tearfully to her father when she went back inside.

Ted gritted his teeth. Causing more bother now, were they? Well, he wouldn't wait much longer . . .

"I thought you were going to clear that sand." Janet Baxter looked accusingly at her husband when he came into the room with his coat on that evening.

"Can't, love. I've got a darts match tonight," he said.

They were almost at the bottom of the league and tonight's match was crucial, so the sand would just have to stay as it was for another night — to Danny's delight if no-one else's.

He had built half a sandcastle by the time his sister Elaine arrived.

She'd called in at her boyfriend's house on her way home to see how he was recuperating from the cold which had kept him away from college that day.

He seemed to be making a remarkable recovery. There was a definite spring in his step as he and that mousey-looking blonde from second-year pottery left his house together, arms entwined.

Pausing now at the gate, she watched her young brother's efforts.

"I can't get the turrets right," he said.

"So I see." Little-brother-type problems were the last thing she wanted to get involved with just then. But seeing the hope in his large, baleful eyes, she sighed and said, "Here, let me have a go."

She crouched down beside him. Somehow, everything she was feeling went into the castle's creation. Under her artistic fingers, it emerged, majestically forlorn, on its mound.

As a finishing touch, Danny tipped his bucket of water round the side of it to form a moat.

Unseen by either of them, Alex Graham had left his own house and was preparing to walk swiftly past them. He glanced at the castle. "Nice." He smiled tentatively.

"Nice? It's fantastic!" Danny declared indignantly.

"All right, it's fantastic," Alex agreed.

Elaine looked up and their eyes met. "Hi," she said in a small voice.

"Hi," Alex said, equally awkwardly. "How's things?"

"Oh, fine." She managed a smile. "How are things at the bank?"

"Boring as ever," Alex said. "Not going out tonight then?"

"No." She spoke casually. "Where are you off to?"

"Oh, I thought I'd see if any of the usual crowd are down the sports centre," Alex said, equally casually. "Haven't seen you there for a while. Not the sporting type then, your friend?"

"Oh, Tim. He's not that much of a friend these days," Elaine said.

"Oh," Alex said. He'd known it wouldn't last. He could spot that type a mile off.

"I'm sorry, Alex. About — well, you know."

"It's all right."

They stood and looked at each other until Danny broke the silence.

"Hey, you're standing on our sand!" he accused Alex.

I DON'T believe it." Sheila Graham looked aghast the following evening when Alex mentioned, somewhat defensively, that he was going out with Elaine. "After the way she's treated you?"

"I'm going, Mum."

"Would you credit that?" Sheila demanded of her husband. "You'll have to do something about it."

"Like what?" Ted demanded. "They're not kids, Sheila!"

Next door, the news that Elaine and Alex were an item again was received with equal consternation by Janet Baxter.

And yet she hated being at loggerheads with the Grahams and couldn't help hoping this might be the first step towards reconciliation.

"He could have made the first move, by helping me clear the sand," Jim said acidly when she made her opinion known. He was still smouldering when he went out to finish the job, and it didn't help when Ted Graham came out of his house all dressed up for going out.

For six weeks Jim hadn't addressed a word to Ted. Yet now, seeing him in his best clothes and convinced he was off to help the Hare and Hounds darts team heap further humiliation on his former team, he couldn't hold his tongue any longer.

"I'd be obliged," he said frostily, "if you'd ask your son to stay away from my daughter."

"Excuse me, but I think you've got that the wrong way round," Ted said. "It's your daughter who's getting her claws into my son again."

Involuntarily, Ted took a step towards Jim as the other man started to speak.

To be fair, he hadn't known about the moat young Danny had made round the castle. And Jim had quite forgotten just where he'd propped his spade.

Disaster overtook both men at precisely the same moment. And, in the confusion of their joint yells, it was understandable that Sheila Graham and Janet Baxter, hearing the commotion and rushing to their respective kitchen windows, should both come to the inevitable, if inaccurate, conclusion.

"They're fighting!" Janet gasped. "Fighting, over Elaine and Alex!"

"Oh no!" Sheila was saying at the same time in her kitchen.

The men looked a sorry sight by the time their wives reached the sand mound. Ted had a bruise on the side of his head where the spade handle had caught him and Jim was lying flat on his back.

"You brute!" Janet screeched, looking at Sheila's husband.

"You idiot!" Sheila yelled, looking at him, too. "When I told you to do something about it, I didn't mean — this . . ." She gestured towards Jim.

"As if there isn't enough violence in the world without you two adding a bit more. You're pathetic!" she added witheringly.

"You could have killed each other!" Janet exclaimed, looking equally appalled. "You don't know your own strength, Jim Baxter. Just look at my Ted's face."

"You look like you could do with a cup of tea, love," Sheila was saying. "Come on inside and I'll make you one."

"Thanks —" Jim broke off when he realised the remark hadn't been addressed to him. He watched, confused, as Sheila took Janet's arm and led her towards their house.

"Men!" he heard her say.

"Yeah — they're all the same," came the other woman's response.

"I think they've ganged up against us, Ted," he said.

Ted was ruefully surveying his stained suit. "Right now," he said, "that's the least of my problems. What am I going to do about this suit?"

"Not much until you get it to the cleaner's," Jim said. "So you may as well get it really filthy by helping me shift this sand."

"It'll cost you a pint," Ted warned. "Oh, by the way, sorry about the other night," he said somewhat sheepishly, recalling the trouncing the Hare and Hounds had given the Rose and Crown.

"Yes, well . . ." Jim bit his lip. Best to let bygones be bygones, particularly as they'd almost certainly be retiring to the Rose and Crown shortly.

"About this sand . . ." Jim frowned. Actually, he wasn't sure now that he wanted a wall in the back garden. He couldn't imagine why he'd thought he did.

I wonder if I can get them to take it back, he mused.

At least the driver would know his way this time, if they did. ∎

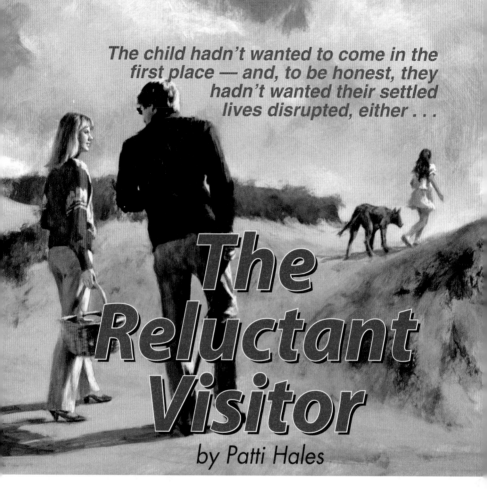

The child hadn't wanted to come in the first place — and, to be honest, they hadn't wanted their settled lives disrupted, either . . .

The Reluctant Visitor

by Patti Hales

GRACE had tried everything. Bribery, cajoling. She'd even attempted threats, although they'd stuck in her throat and made her feel guilty.

Nothing had worked so far. Not kindness, not a quick hug, not even the breakfast cereal, which Natasha had vowed was the only one she'd eat, but which remained in her blue-striped bowl, untouched, morning after morning.

Elbows on the table, unbrushed dark hair hanging in tangled ringlets, Natasha's expression was unfathomable. Grace's desperate attempts at any kind of conversation rarely evoked any response.

This morning had been the last straw.

"So how long do I have to stay in this dump?" she'd asked, swinging her thin legs and kicking viciously at the stripped pine chair.

The question had set Grace's teeth on edge. "Come on, Natasha, it's not that bad.

"And you like the beach, don't you?"

As far as she'd been able to tell, Natasha had enjoyed the new experience.

Whoops of laughter had rung out as she'd pranced through the playful waves. For short spells the awful, haunted look had disappeared from the proud little face.

She'd looked like any other little girl as she'd mastered the art of skimming flat stones across the water and counting the bounces.

"Did you see that, Auntie Grace? That was a seven." A couple of peanut butter sandwiches had disappeared down the small throat. A packet of cheese and onion crisps and a chocolate biscuit had followed. "Next one will be an eight. Bet you a million pounds."

At times like that, Grace had been filled with hope. A bit of patience — that was all that was required.

"She looks a lot healthier," Sam had remarked after Natasha had gone up to bed one night. "And so do you," he'd added with a smile.

Grace had wrinkled her lightly-tanned nose and grinned.

"At least I'm getting plenty of exercise. I didn't realise just how demanding kids could be, but you're right. It's doing us both a power of good."

Now it appeared to Grace that she'd been wrong.

"You do enjoy the beach, don't you?" she'd repeated. "We have a lovely time there, don't we?"

"Who says?" Natasha had retorted. "And if you really want to know, I'm bored stiff!" With that, she'd flounced out.

Part of Grace had wanted to hit back with an equally acid retort, to yell after the girl about how she ought to be grateful that she'd been made so welcome and how there must be millions of children who'd give everything for what Natasha was taking so much for granted.

But what good would it do?

The child clearly detested her — and Sam. The life they lived was nothing like the one she'd been used to.

Lying awake, night after night, she'd alternated between vowing to pack her niece's bags first thing in the morning and trying harder to understand the girl's behaviour.

Understanding. That was the secret. And patience, lots and lots of patience. It had only been less than three months since Natasha's life had changed out of all recognition. Eleven short weeks.

The calmer Grace could stay, the sooner the healing process would begin, for all of them.

Lydia and Ryan hadn't perhaps been the most conventional of parents, but they'd adored their daughter and each other. The accident had been no-one's fault. A patch of unexpected black ice . . .

Grace still found it hard to accept that Lydia had gone.

Even if they hadn't been that close, it still hurt to know that she'd lost her only sister . . .

130

And if she found it hard, then Natasha's emotions must be in deep turmoil.

She was a townie. Born and bred. She'd been used to shopping centres, cinema complexes and no end of trendy clothes.

Unpacking the designer suitcase, Grace had pulled a face. Lycra leggings . . . skimpy, glittery tops . . . little mini-skirts? For heaven's sake — the girl was only nine.

How on earth she was supposed to play in this kind of gear, Grace hadn't begun to imagine.

Surely a couple of pairs of jeans, some T-shirts, maybe a pretty dress or two, would have been much more suitable?

All the old resentment she'd felt against her sister had bubbled up inside her. Firmly she pushed it down.

THE phone call had come out of the blue. Natasha's grandmother had sounded at the end of her tether.

"I know you and your sister weren't that close, but Natasha is your niece, Grace," she'd said plaintively, "and if I don't get a break, I don't know what I'll do. She's not the easiest of little girls to cope with."

Instantly, Grace had known exactly what she'd meant. The few times she'd been in Natasha's company, she'd been secretly horrified.

If she'd been closer to Lydia, she might have said something, only their relationship hadn't been like that. Lydia would have instantly put her down. Said something like: "Oh yes . . . and since when have you been an expert on the subject?" Or, "They're all the same at this stage. You're such an old fusspot, Grace."

Her first instincts had been to refuse even to entertain the idea. It wouldn't be fair on anyone, she'd thought. Not on her, not on Sam and certainly not on Natasha.

She knew absolutely nothing about children. Not through choice, though.

She and Sam, in the early days of their marriage, had talked endlessly about how they'd fill their home with a huge family. A boy for you and a girl for me, they'd joked.a

"There are other things in life besides having children." The specialist had been kind, but brusque.

Grace had felt at that point as if her heart would finally break.

Only it hadn't and she'd tried desperately not to let Sam see just how deep her pain really went.

"It's no-one's fault," she'd kept telling herself over the years. And she couldn't deny there were advantages; foreign holidays, eating out whenever they felt like it, no sticky fingermarks on the pale paintwork.

If, and it was a big if, she agreed to take on her orphaned niece, then all that would change overnight. And, deep down, she doubted her own capabilities.

The only time she'd been left in charge of a small creature it had been of the easy-care variety. A gentle lop-eared rabbit with silky amber hair and round, trusting eyes.

When Grace had picked it up, the plump body had snuggled trustingly against her. She'd been sad to return him to his owner after the holidays.

But Natasha wasn't a rabbit. A hedgehog might be a better way to describe the prickly child.

In the end, and because Sam wasn't around to discuss the situation with, Grace had agreed to take Natasha for a trial period. . .

"Right, then." The relief in the older woman's voice was almost tangible. "I'll deliver her to you tomorrow."

Deliver . . . like a parcel. And tomorrow . . . Grace had poured herself a glass of sherry. Sympathy for the — it seemed — unwanted little girl swept through her, like a determined wave surging over the sand.

"It'll be all right." She'd said the words out loud, over and over again, as she'd prepared a bedroom for Natasha.

BUT it hadn't been all right. In fact, it had been all wrong from the very moment the child had walked through the front door. Grace had realised immediately that Natasha was going to be difficult.

"She'll settle down." Her grandmother had said exactly that as she'd kissed the child goodbye. Sam had echoed the words a few days later.

But Natasha hadn't settled down. In fact, she'd seemed to delight in finding new ways to test her aunt's patience.

"Would you prefer to go back to your grandma's?" Grace had asked one day, when a sullen Natasha had come down for lunch.

"Don't care where I go." The reply had been accompanied by a tiny gleam in the little girl's eyes. A victory gleam.

Grace clattered the plates together.

When Sam came in tonight, she'd tell him. Together they could ring Ryan's mother. She wouldn't be over the moon, but she was Natasha's legal guardian after all.

Relieved that things would soon be back to normal, she allowed Natasha to watch cartoon videos all afternoon.

Grace was in the kitchen grilling sausages when she heard Sam's car pull up. Checking that Natasha was still glued to the screen, she dashed outside.

Her eyes widened at the sight of the sleek dark head and huge brown eyes staring at her dolefully from the rear window.

Sam looked awkward, his smile unsure. "I don't know if this is a good idea or not . . ."

Grace could feel her lower jaw drop. There wasn't a single thing she could do to stop it. "What is that?" Her words came out in a high, whispery sound.

"He answers to the unlikely name of Bartholomew." Gingerly, Sam opened the rear passenger door and the dog sprang out. After giving Grace a quick once over, he sat right in front of her and solemnly raised one paw.

"Who does he belong to?" Grace sank on to one knee. A cross Labrador, she guessed. Not much more than a couple of years old, judging by the clear eyes and pure white teeth showing in a neat row beside a lolling pink tongue.

She stood up. The dog mimicked her action, pressing his head against her thigh.

Sam's arm slid round her waist. "No-one. That's the problem. A chap at work took him on, but his wife couldn't stand dog hairs all over the place. She said he had to go.

"When he told me that, I wondered if it might help things here if we took him. In a way he reminds me of —"

"— Natasha," Grace interrupted.

Sam nodded. "I thought — hoped — she might find a kindred spirit in this chap." He looked deep into Grace's eyes. "But you don't, do you?"

If the dog had been an elegant poodle she thought, then he might have a point.

This scruffy chap, who was nuzzling at her hand for attention, would only be something else for Natasha to turn her nose up at.

"Quite frankly," Grace began, "I was going to have a talk with you later. I honestly don't think —" She stopped as the dog hurled himself towards the open door and a watchful Natasha.

For a split second, the girl's eyes sparkled. Momentarily, her hand reached out, then she snatched it back.

"What an ugly creature!" she sniffed haughtily and glared at Grace. "And he smells," she added, turning her back.

Head on one side, Bartholomew squatted down. He turned and looked pathetically at Grace. That look spurred her into action. Natasha might not have found a friend, but she was fairly certain that she had. And she knew instinctively that he would adore the beach.

"Come on, boy. Let's see if we can find you some supper."

Sam chuckled. "Him or me?"

"Since I don't have any canine cuisine, he'll have to slum it and settle for chicken casserole. There might," she teased, "even be enough for you, too!"

NATASHA maintained her stony silence throughout the meal. Now and again her eyes strayed towards the window and out into the garden where the dog was happily sniffing round his new territory, but when she caught Grace watching her, she returned to pushing her food round and round her plate.

"I'm tired," she announced suddenly. "I'm going to bed."

Seeing Sam about to comment on this unusual occurrence, Grace shook her head wildly. She needed this time alone with him.

"Out with it," Sam said, as the house vibrated to the slam of Natasha's bedroom door.

Grace pushed her own uneaten meal to one side. She took a deep breath. "I'm admitting defeat. Nothing works, Sam, absolutely nothing! She loathes me, looks at me as if I'm the wicked queen from a fairy story.

"And the worst thing is . . ." Grace's eyes filled with tears, "the very worst thing is that I'm beginning to dislike her, too . . . I — I don't like admitting I've failed her . . . but —" she gulped "— that's how it is, Sam . . ."

Sam's hand closed round her own trembling one. "If it's any consolation at all, sweetheart, I feel exactly the same. I've been trying to find the right way to broach the subject." He shrugged helplessly. "At least we can console ourselves that we tried."

His eyes looked towards the ceiling. "That's not a child up there — that's a fully-fledged monster."

On and off all evening, despair turning to desperation, time and again Grace punched out Natasha's grandmother's telephone number. "You don't think she's gone off somewhere, away from all this, do you?" she asked Sam, at midnight.

He smiled wryly. "I wouldn't really blame her, under the circumstances.

Grace tossed and turned all night. Her sister's accusing face kept coming into her mind.

Giving up all hope of even an hour's release, Grace slid out of bed. A cup of tea and a read of the paper Sam had brought home would pass some of the long hours until dawn.

There was no sound coming from the utility room. Good. At least Bartholomew seemed to have settled happily into his new surroundings.

Carrying the cup into the living-room, she flopped into the chair and tucked her legs underneath her. The comics she'd bought for Natasha lay, unread, in a pile on the coffee-table. They seemed only to accentuate her failure to reach the child.

Restlessly, Grace stood up and walked over to draw back the curtains. Immediately, her eyes were drawn to the gap where the patio doors didn't quite meet. How could that have happened?

She'd locked up. She always did. It was second nature, regardless of the circumstances.

It was then that she heard the low voice coming from the garden.

"Actually," Natasha was saying, "they're very nice. Auntie Grace is very kind. She's a good cook, too. And Uncle Sam knows all sorts of things. He's great. You'll like him."

Grace couldn't believe what she was hearing. Or work out who on earth the child was talking to. But Natasha's next words clarified the situation.

"But if you take my advice, Bartholomew, you won't let yourself love them. Loving people is a stupid thing to do. Sometimes they die, you see, and even if they don't . . . they don't always love you back."

It took every ounce of Grace's self-control not to barge in. Her body rigid, she waited.

"I'm not really sure if my mum and dad loved me . . . They were never there . . . they were always busy. I had nannies, of course, but they didn't really care either. They let me do anything I wanted . . . because they were getting paid for it . . . and we did have a beautiful house . . .

"Not as nice as this one . . . it was in town so we weren't near a beach or anything."

A faint smile passed across Grace's tense face. She'd been right about one thing, after all. Hugging her body, she listened as Natasha's voice, louder now, filled the still, early morning air.

"So my advice is just to do what you want. They won't stop you. They won't make you go to bed or eat your dinner, or anything.

"They won't tell you to behave yourself and that's because they don't really care, you see. And when they get fed up with you, they'll pass you on to someone else.

"We can be friends for now, if you like, but we mustn't tell them. And I'm sorry I said you were ugly and smelly. You're not. You're absolutely beautiful and I could really, really love you."

Although the sun couldn't rise at two in the morning, Grace could feel a warmth touch her damp cheeks.

There would be no telephone call. But there would be rules from now on. Natasha would have to learn to toe the line, but she'd also learn that she was entitled to love, and that she'd receive all the loving care that Grace and Sam could give her.

The battle hadn't been won . . . but the first healing rays had risen over the top of the barriers. ■

More Than Memories

by Cheryl Morgan

In looking back to happy, family days, she'd forgotten how much she had to look forward to . . .

'M glad you persuaded me to sort this cupboard out, Mum. I've found tons of stuff I thought I'd lost." Janet handed her son, Mark a carrier bag and he began to cram things into it, his expression reminiscent of a child on Christmas Day.

She could almost see the child he had been now, gathering up his presents and whisking them away upstairs, to be appreciated at leisure later.

But Mark wasn't a child any more, and he wasn't whisking them away upstairs.

"Would you like a cup of tea before you go?" she asked.

"Go on then, just a quick one. I'm picking Ellie up from the hairdresser's at twelve."

"How is Ellie?"

"Fine." His eyes gleamed. "Happy — we both are."

Mark was happy, that was all that mattered. She'd said as much to her husband, Graham, last night.

"Ellie's a smashing girl," she'd said. But . . ." Her voice had drifted off wistfully. "When Joanna left home it happened gradually. First there was the engagement, then the wedding to arrange. I had time to imagine what it was going to be like without her.

"This has happened too quickly. Four weeks ago, Mark bowled into the lounge and said, 'Ellie and I have decided to get a flat together,' Then, a fortnight later, he was gone."

"It's just the way they do it these days, love. We were lucky with Joanna," Graham said.

"And that's another thing. Do you realise Joanna and Paul have only visited us once since Mark left?"

"Really? Surely you don't think there's a connection?"

"I don't know." Janet reached for his hand. "I just feel that, all at once, everything's happening somewhere else."

Why was it so difficult to explain? She worked four mornings a week in the college library, had plenty of friends, went swimming on Tuesday evenings, enjoyed a good book. None of that had changed.

It was the backcloth to her life which had deserted her so suddenly — the bit that gave it purpose.

"TEA'S ready, Mark," Janet called to the hallway, from where muffled clunks and bangs could still be heard as Mark raked through the memories of the past.

"Cheers, Mum."

It was good to have him here, Janet thought. She'd wondered, when she'd rung him first thing and suggested he come round and sort out the cupboard under the stairs, whether he'd say he had better ways to spend his Saturday morning.

"So, what have you been up to all week?" she asked.

"Decorating."

"You? Decorating?"

Mark looked hurt. "I'm pretty good at it actually. We had a bit of trouble with the ceiling, though."

Janet smiled. "Tricky things, ceilings. Have you seen Joanna and Paul?"

"They've popped in a couple of times."

"How are they?"

"Fine."

His reply seemed evasive — or had she imagined it?

★★★★

Janet climbed the stairs. Below, a door slammed shut. She stopped and looked down. Mark was standing in the hall, looking tousled and a little out of breath.

"The car won't start," he said. "Mum, you couldn't do me a favour, could you?"

The door again, opening quietly, closing with a slam. Only one person ever closed doors like that.

"Hi there. Anybody home?" Joanna's voice rang through the house.

"Ah, there you are." She dug her brother in the ribs. "You haven't told her, have you?"

"Of course I haven't. Look, Jo, you couldn't tell her later, could you? The car won't start. I need Mum to pick Ellie up from the hairdresser's."

"Ellie can wait five minutes."

Janet, still standing halfway up the stairs, felt slightly bemused.

"Paul can go and get Ellie." Joanna flung open the front door and peered out. "Oh, drat. He's gone already."

"Tell me what?" Janet asked in exasperation at the way the conversation was flowing all around her.

Joanna turned to her and took a deep breath.

"I'm pregnant," she said simply. "I've suspected I was for ages, but I wanted to be sure before I told you. That's why I haven't been round much lately. I couldn't trust myself not to blurt it out."

"Mu-um!" Playfully, Mark clapped a hand over his sister's mouth, stopping her in mid-flow. "This is an emergency! Never mind Joanna's baby. If Ellie isn't picked up soon, we could have a family funeral on our hands!

"Ple-ease . . . It'll only take five minutes."

"Rat!" his sister squealed, and tickled him. The two of them tussled for a moment, then stopped, laughing.

Janet shook her head at the pair of them. For all that they were grown-up now, they were still kids at heart. Nothing had really changed. Maybe they weren't around all the time, but they were still her children, and they always would be.

In a sudden swell of delight, she ran down the stairs and hugged her daughter.

"You've still got the cot in the attic, haven't you?" Joanna asked. "I want Junior to get used to staying with his granny right from the start."

"Poor Mum, she isn't going to know what hit her."

"Mum'll love it, won't you Mum?"

"Yes, darling, of course I will."

"But what about picking up Ellie? Mum . . . Please!"

Janet raised her hands for silence. They stood, heads down, hands clasped in contrition, like the obedient children they'd never really been.

Janet grinned.

"First, I'll pick up Ellie," she said. "I've just about got time."

Their heads shot up enquiringly.

"I'm meeting your dad for lunch. Then we're going shopping, and this evening we'll be stripping the paper off the bedroom ceiling.

"But if you'd all like to come round tomorrow for Sunday dinner, we'll have some time to talk."

"I wanted Dad to help me fix the car tomorrow." Mark looked disgruntled.

"And I thought you and I could have a look round the baby shops," Joanna added.

Janet lifted her car-keys from the hook. Something deep inside her seemed to settle into place.

This must have been how Mark had felt, she thought, when he emerged from the cupboard, his arms crammed full of all those things he thought he'd lost.

But it was more than that.

"Paul can help you with the car when he comes back for Joanna," she told her son. "And we'll have a look round all the baby stores next week, love."

Then she kissed them both, giving Joanna an extra little squeeze.

"I expect you'll be gone by the time your dad and I get back," she said. "But we'll see you all tomorrow, yes?"

"Yes."

Janet closed the door quietly behind her and hurried to the car.

She felt like a child on Christmas Day who has gone downstairs in the morning to see only one box under the tree, but on opening it, has discovered that it contains hundreds of smaller boxes, each with a magical surprise inside.

Her life now was a bit like that, she thought. There were so many new treasures to look forward to — things she had never anticipated.

Being a granny would be one of them, of course, but she'd caught a glimpse of quite a few others.

"Who knows what the future may bring," she said to herself as she settled down in the car and started the engine. "Today, the bedroom ceiling; tomorrow, perhaps, that Caribbean island . . ." ■

She was risking all she held dear for a man
she barely knew . . .

Playing With Fire

by Isobel Stewart

JOANNA was never sure, afterwards, when it was that she began to question her marriage. In the early days, when they were both working, the times they had together, away from the hospital, were so special that the times apart didn't matter.

But that, she thought all these years later, was long ago, and it seemed to her now that she and Clive were two strangers.

It hadn't always been like this. Even through the unbelievably busy and noisy years of having two babies only 18 months apart, there had still been that magic and loving bond between them.

Now, suddenly — and somehow it did seem a sudden and immediate happening, not a gradual one — life had become more ordered, more civilised.

Lindy was ten, and Peter would soon be nine; they were two separate, independent little people. There was the opportunity now for Joanna to spend time working in the garden, time to think — and time for her to begin to question her marriage . . .

It was a good marriage, she told herself. There was laughter, there was love, there was warmth.

And yet — and yet . . .

Something indefinable that had been there in these early years had gone. She didn't know when it had gone, she just knew that it was no longer there.

Clive was a G.P. now, and they had always known there would be constant demands on his time, but that didn't make coping with the reality any easier.

She hadn't foreseen the reality of a family picnic, long planned, and then a telephone call, leaving Joanna and the children alone at the beach.

Or a film they both wanted to see, and Clive's bleeper sounding halfway through, so that Joanna saw the second half alone.

And so many dinner parties ended with Joanna going there, or returning home, on her own, or entertaining friends on her own, with Clive's chair empty.

Most of all, though, it was the loss of family time that she minded. And she found herself thinking, more and more, that it would have helped if it had seemed to matter as much to Clive as it did to her.

There were, of course, she reminded herself fairly, many times when there were no demands from patients, when their time together, as the two of them, or with the children, was uninterrupted.

But more and more she found that she was forging a life by herself. In many ways, that was a good thing, she knew that, but still it bothered her.

It wasn't as if she didn't love Clive, or even doubted his love for her. It was just — a questioning, a looking back at what their marriage had been, and at what it was now.

IT was a busy winter, with a flu epidemic, and Clive's practice had increased dramatically. Both the children went down with flu a few days later, and Joanna nursed them through it, refusing to go down with it herself, because she knew she couldn't. At the end, however, she felt drained and weary.

Perhaps, she thought later, it was the aftermath of the flu she refused to have that gave her a strange feeling of remoteness from the rest of the world.

This feeling of being out of touch with everyone else almost stopped her going to dinner with friends a few nights later, when Clive was called away. But in the end, with the babysitter already on her way, she decided to go through with it.

"Poor Clive," her friend Madge said, when Joanna made her apologies for him. "Still, never mind. Tom's brought the new fellow from the bank. He's just moved here. He was divorced last year. Seems quite nice."

Richard Payne was nice. He was also a pretty good conversationalist, and before long he and Joanna were engaged in a spirited discussion on the environment.

As Joanna drove home later that evening, the feeling of being apart from the world had completely disappeared.

A FEW days later, Joanna was unloading her shopping from the trolley into her car when she heard her name, and turned round to see Richard Payne.

"Joanna — this is lucky! Here, let me help you."

He lifted the rest of the bags, put them in the car, and then took the key from her and locked the boot.

"Now," he said, briskly, "come and have a cup of coffee with me."

Joanna hesitated.

"Come on," Richard said. "If you'd met Madge, you'd have gone. Surely this is just the same?"

"Of course it is," Joanna agreed, knowing that it most certainly wasn't the same.

"Just a quick cup, though, Richard. I have to get back home and I'm sure you're in a hurry too."

It was an hour before they came out of the little coffee shop.

Joanna, surprised and a little guilty at how much she'd enjoyed herself, couldn't believe the time.

What had they talked about, she asked herself, as she drove home. They'd touched briefly on his divorce — the only good thing being that there were no children to be hurt by it — and he'd asked about her family, but surely that couldn't have taken an hour!

"Whatever . . ." she told herself. "It's perfectly harmless — good for me, in fact. He makes me see myself in a different light, that's all."

That different light continued to make life interesting once the lassitude of winter disappeared.

Joanna took the children for unexpected picnics; she took the dog to training classes; she made new curtains for the house. She went back to yoga, and had her hair cut.

"You're very bright these days, love," Clive said unexpectedly one day. "And I like your hair like that. That's the way it was when I first knew you."

Joanna suppressed a bubble of laughter, for apart from the fact that her hair had been short then, and was short now, there was no real resemblance.

But she didn't mind, because it was sweet of Clive of have noticed, and she sat on the arm of his chair and kissed his ear. He looked surprised, but pleased, and returned the kiss with interest.

If knowing Richard makes me feel this good, and makes me a nicer and brighter wife and mother, there's no harm in it, she told herself reasonably.

Not that she met him or saw him often — occasionally at dinner parties, once at their own house, when miraculously Clive wasn't called out, once or twice at the shopping centre, with time for no more than a few words.

And once, when she was walking the dog down beside the river, Richard's car stopped beside her, and he got out and took Skip's lead from her, and then stood watching while she put the dog through his various commands. And that was all, really.

Joanna knew that there was nothing serious in these pleasant little encounters, for either of them.

But she knew, too, with equal certainty, that there was a spark of attraction between them. And in her most honest moments, she had to admit to herself that it was this knowledge that made her everyday world suddenly so much more exciting.

And if that made her brighter for everyone around her, then what could be wrong with it? Nothing at all, she told herself firmly.

And that lasted until the day Peter burnt his hand.

SHE and Clive were having a quick cup of coffee on a Saturday morning, just before Clive left for surgery, when they heard a scream from the garage and Lindy came running in.

"Peter's hurt his hand!" she gasped. "Come quickly, he burned it."

When they reached the garage, Peter, white and in tears, held out his hand, with an ugly burn on it.

When the small hurt hand was bandaged, Peter was sitting, still white and shaken, drinking a cup of hot sweet tea.

"Oh, Peter," Joanna said, not quite steadily. "Just sit quietly and drink your tea, then I think you should lie down for a bit, and —"

"Just a minute, Joanna."

She looked at Clive, taken aback by the severity of his voice.

"Now, Peter," he said quietly. "I want to know how this happened."

Peter swallowed and instinctively her arm tightened around him.

But something in Clive's eyes, holding hers, made her stop and leave Peter to face his father on his own.

"I wanted to see how it would look in the garage with no lights on, and just a candle," the boy said, shakily. "So I lit the candle, and Lindy put the lights out, and — and I think some of the wax dripped on my hand.

"So I dropped the candle, and that was when it burned me."

Clive looked at his son, not saying anything, and at last Peter's gaze dropped to the floor.

"You know the rules about using matches, Peter." Clive's voice was quiet, firm. "And maybe now you know why we make these rules.

"You burned your hand, but you might just as easily have set fire to the garage, because lighting matches in a place where there is petrol is very irresponsible, and very dangerous."

"I'm sorry, Daddy," Peter muttered, his face whiter than ever.

"Clive, he's only eight, and his hand is very painful . . . Surely —" Joanna began, unable to keep silent.

"Surely nothing," Clive replied brusquely. "All right, Peter, I've nothing else to say."

Both children went out of the room, white and subdued, but at the door, Peter turned.

"I'm sorry," he said again.

"Yes, I should hope so," Clive returned. "Just make sure you don't ever again do anything as stupid and as dangerous."

The door closed.

"You were pretty hard on him," Joanna protested.

"I had to be," Clive replied, and she saw now that he was white as well. "Joanna, he's old enough to know that playing with fire is dangerous."

"You're right, of course," Joanna agreed, after a moment. "But a little sympathy wouldn't have gone amiss."

"I'm sorry, but I don't agree," Clive said quietly. "Peter knew what he was doing and he knew it was wrong. He has to learn to take responsibility for his own actions."

He smiled thinly. "But I must admit it wasn't easy for me to be so hard on him — it never is when it's someone you love who is hurt."

144

He looked at his watch. "I'm late — should be back around lunchtime."

He kissed the top of her head. But at the door, he stopped.

"Joanna?" he said. "You do understand why I had to be tough with Peter?"

It was a moment before she replied.

"Yes," she said, slowly, meaning it. "Yes, Clive, I understand."

FOR the first time for so long, she stood at the window, watching as he reversed the car out of the drive. She didn't know whether he had seen her or not, but she waved, just in case.

Yes, she thought, I do understand; maybe better than you realise. I've been playing with fire, too, and I am certainly old enough to know better.

I was fed up with all the demands made on Clive, and I was forgetting that this life was my choice, too. I wasn't taking responsibility for that.

Seeing Richard was fun, and it was exciting, but it was irresponsible, and potentially dangerous.

It would have to stop, she knew that. But she knew, too, that she couldn't just push out of sight the things that had made her question their marriage in the first place.

They would have to do some thinking, and some talking, she and Clive.

She would tell him how she had felt. She would admit that she had so often come close to real resentment of the demands of his job. And not only the job, but the fact that he didn't seem to mind these demands.

Perhaps Clive could consider going into partnership, sharing his calls on his time.

Perhaps, too, she should think about going back to nursing work, even part-time. It would give her something to channel her energies into.

Over the years, she looked back on that long-ago Joanna and Clive, those two young people who had seemed like strangers, and she realised that they weren't strangers at all. They were still inside each of them.

The important thing, now, was that she had to be honest with herself — about Richard, about Clive, about their marriage.

It was, as she had always known, a good marriage. But a marriage both she and Clive had perhaps taken for granted.

Joanna turned away from the window.

I've come close to burning my fingers she thought. But I know for certain that I'm finished playing with fire . . .■

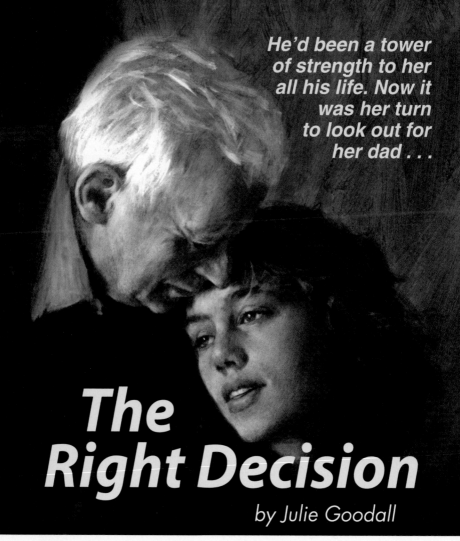

He'd been a tower of strength to her all his life. Now it was her turn to look out for her dad . . .

The Right Decision

by Julie Goodall

STACEY eased the car door gently shut, reluctant to break the peace and tranquillity of the housing estate where her father lived.

Not for the first time, Stacey felt glad that her father had been able to spend so many happy years here.

That thought brought another to the forefront of her mind: that those years, so many of them spent happily with her mother, were about to come to an end.

"Charles, this is the right thing to do, isn't it? Dad will like it at Greenfields?"

Her husband slipped a hand encouragingly into hers.

"Of course he will, love. And the most important thing is that he'll be safe."

Stacey nodded, clinging to his hand as they made their way up the path. It was three o'clock in the afternoon and there was still a bottle of milk on the step. Her father wouldn't be needing it now, she thought ruefully.

In half an hour he would be leaving his home for the very last time, to begin a new life at Greenfields, a nursing home for the elderly on the outskirts of the town.

Stacey looked around the bungalow that had once been her home. Everything was exactly as she'd left it the previous day — even the magazine that she'd brought him lay, apparently untouched, on the table in the centre of the small room.

To her dismay, she noticed that her father was wearing the same set of clothes.

"Have you eaten, Pop?" Charles asked, crouched right down to his level, gently covering one of Matthew's hands with his own.

"Baked beans," the old man muttered.

The waste bin showed no sign of anything having been opened and the kettle felt cold to the touch.

"Ready then, Dad?" Stacey announced lightly. Her father had risen and the sight of him standing, silhouetted by the bay window, made her task easier than she'd anticipated.

His frame was bent over and thin — so unlike the huge, strong figure that he had been all through her childhood.

Now it was her turn to do the caring. To give her father what he desperately needed, but was unable to do for himself.

Stacey crossed the room and took her father's hands in her own.

"Ready then?" she asked.

The blank look on his face made her heart sink.

"Where are we going?" was his reply.

"We've found you a new home, remember?" she said, stroking his soft cheek with the back of her hand.

A frown increased the crinkles in Matthew's brow.

"I didn't have time to read it," he told her, sadly, nodding towards the magazine on the coffee table.

"It doesn't matter, Dad," she told him softly. The eyes gazed back trustingly into her own.

"No time," he muttered quietly.

"I brought you this," she told him, kissing him on the cheek. "A present. A book. I know how much you love reading."

FOR a moment, she looked at the bookcases lining the familiar room, remembering a time when her father would have sat reading night after night.

A flicker of recognition flashed across his age-worn features as he opened the package with trembling hands. It was his favourite author, Hammond Innes.

"That's the cases," Charles announced, placing two suitcases by the front door. "Are we ready then?"

Nobody spoke, and Stacey fixed her gaze on the swirling pattern of the hall carpet. Charles, slightly uncomfortable, cleared his throat.

"Come on, then," Matthew insisted unexpectedly, picking up a case as he made his way out of the front door.

Then he paused.

"We've forgotten something." He stood for a moment, seeming to reach within himself for the answer. "Sybil."

"Oh, Dad."

Stacey caught him up quickly, placing her arm around his stooped shoulders.

"Mum died six years ago. Remember?"

For a moment, poignant memories of her mother pervaded her thoughts, then she forced herself to let them go. Matthew walked on ahead, the hint of a shrug complementing the confusion etched on his face.

It makes it easier, somehow, Stacey thought. To see him this way was so painful, but it did serve to confirm that what she and Charles were doing was for the best.

Her father sat, silent, in the back of the car, the book clutched tightly in his hand.

Stacey looked at her watch. 3.30 p.m. They were prompt, and Mrs Hall, the matron, stepped out of the entrance.

"Welcome, Mr Lynton," she said kindly, helping Matthew from the car.

"I think we've left Sybil behind."

"Oh, I'm sure you haven't," she reassured him, gesturing for Stacey and Charles to follow with the cases.

Inside, a small comfortable hall led into a larger lounge. Everywhere smelled of freshly-cut flowers and there was a friendly atmosphere about the place and all the occupants appeared relaxed and settled. Now that they had arrived, she felt certain that her father would feel at home here.

"Would you like to see your room, Mr Lynton?" Mrs Hall asked, but Matthew had wandered off to look out of a window into the vast green garden beyond. Stacey saw that he still held the book in his hand.

"I'll sit here for a while," he announced, with surprising certainty. He'd chosen a chair with a decisiveness which reminded her of his earlier years — a huge armchair, which almost engulfed his delicate body. He called his daughter to his side. "Where's Sybil?"

"You can't see her any more, Dad," she whispered softly. "But she's with you, I promise. She'll always be with you, wherever you are."

STACEY smiled through damp misty vision at the childish surprise in his voice as he opened his book.

"I'll have time to read this now, then," he said, looking up.

"You certainly will."

"Are you crying, Stace?"

Strangely, for that instant, he was her reliable father once more, wondering how she was feeling, ready to offer his help. Then, the drifting expression returned.

"I'm just pleased for you, Dad. That you've got all the time you want to read."

"I enjoy reading."

"I know."

She remembered the hours he'd spent reading aloud to her when she was a child. Perhaps, in the future, it would be her turn to read aloud to her father.

"Mrs Hall is putting your things in your room, Dad. We've got to pop off and do a little shopping before the shops shut, but then we'll be back after you've had your tea to see how you've settled in. Is that all right?"

But she'd lost him. The book open, Hammond Innes had drawn him into an imaginary world, taking him back to the years in the Navy when he'd fought for King and Country. Silently, Stacey slipped away.

"We'll be back in a short while," she told Mrs Hall. "Just to check that he's settling in OK."

"You're very welcome," she told them, "but he certainly looks at home already to me."

"He'll be fine," Charles told her with a reassuring hug. "This is just what he needs."

"I know." Stacey sighed. "It's just hard at first — leaving him. Come on. We'll pop in again later."

Leading the way, she was unable to resist a last peek through the window and there he was, holding his new book aloft, showing it off to another resident of the home. No doubt he was already relating tales of his years of active service, Stacey thought with a smile.

"See you later, Dad," she whispered, drawing comfort from the pair of old gloves in her pocket. "And 'bye, Mum," she added with a hint of a smile.

Charles revved up and pulled away out of the long gravel drive. ■

A New Image

*. . . was needed to go with her
dream dress — and Alice set to
the task with great gusto!*

by Patti Hales

HERE I am . . . crutches bedecked with jade and silver ribbons . . .
the vestiges of my black eye not completely concealed under
several layers of make-up . . . waiting for Jamie to collect me by
taxi.

My rather ornately-autographed plaster stretches from ankle to
thigh.

On the plus side, I no longer have to wear a collar to support my
neck, and my fingernails are the best they've ever been: long,
perfectly oval and varnished a glowing apricot colour. Perfect to show
off a two-in-a-twist diamond ring.

But still, it's not exactly how I'd hoped to present myself on this most romantic of occasions . . .

My troubles, or maybe I should say misfortunes, had all started over something as potentially innocent as a dress. Mind you, this is no ordinary dress.

It's an absolute dream of a creation; midnight blue crêpe, with an off-the-shoulder neckline, and star-shaped, cut-out bits at the waistline. Perfect for my engagement party!

Close-up, the creation was even more stunning. And draped round the sculpted hem was a selection of perfectly-matching accessories: shoes, bag, fabulous earrings.

The slender sales woman surveyed me professionally. "Size fourteen is the largest we have in that style. Perhaps — "

"Fourteen's fine," I'd interrupted swiftly. "In fact, I've got several twelves in my wardrobe." That they hadn't fitted me in five years was neither here nor there.

Now I'd be lying if I said that the dress and I had been made for each other. If it was a size 14, it was a skimpy 14. The shoes were perfect, though. Like walking on air. And the earrings shimmered and caught the light every time I moved my head a single degree.

"I'll take it," I'd said. "And the other bits, too," I'd carried on, mentally working out that I'd pay by cheque, then transfer money from my building society into the bank.

BACK out in the High Street and reeling from the cost, I walked past the deli. The long chocolate éclairs in the window had seemed to be laughing at me. It might have been a trick of the light, but the way the tomatoes had been arranged on top of the rows of quiches looked as if they spelled out my name — and a little message. ALICE. Like my namesake from Wonderland. EAT ME.

"Can't afford you any more," I'd hissed and, filled with determination, had popped into the supermarket for a carton of low-fat Greek yoghurt and a huge slice of water melon.

On the way out of the store I'd spent my last few pounds until pay day on a couple of slimming magazines with enticing headlines: I'M HALF THE WOMAN I USED TO BE and EXERCISE YOUR WAY TO A BEAUTIFUL BODY.

Exercise! I'd physically shuddered at the very thought. Swimsuits, in my book, were garments designed to ensure maximum tanning possibilities. And as for running round a squash court, sweaty and panting for every single breath . . .

Quite frankly, I'd almost given up at that point.

Then the vision of how I could look . . . in the dress . . . had raced to the rescue.

THAT afternoon, when my boss had gone to a meeting, I'd rung the local sports centre and made an appointment for a personal assessment from one of their fitness trainers.

"Make sure it's a tough programme," I'd told the receptionist recklessly. "I've only got eight weeks."

"They're all tough," she'd said flatly.

I'll spare you the details of what I suffered over the next month. Suffice to say that I lost 17 pounds and found bones I'd never realised the average human being possessed.

Eating sensibly had become second nature. And I'd never felt better.

Sonia, my trainer, was tremendously encouraging, and when I'd asked Jamie what he thought of the change in me, he'd nodded vaguely and said, "Great."

As for the dress . . . every time I slid into it, it looked better and better. And there were still another four weeks to go!

WHEN are we going to see it?" Mum had asked one evening, trying to hide her bacon sandwich under a rumpled sheet of kitchen towel.

"Two more weeks," I'd told her, tucking into ribbon pasta with a fresh tomato dressing.

By then I reckoned I'd be home and dry. Able to cut down on the strict regime of step-aerobics, jazz-dancing and weight training.

Naturally, I'd stick with my new eating plan, but with the occasional day off for a doorstep of melted cheese, oozing between two doorsteps of unhealthy white toast.

★★★★

The days passed quickly. Fortunately, Jamie was having to dedicate more and more time to studying for his final exams and so he didn't actually notice how many hours I was spending on the final firming-up process.

Ultimately the big night had arrived.

With the entire family waiting downstairs, I'd stepped on to the bathroom scales. Twenty five pounds had gone wherever fat goes when it's no longer required.

The dress had slid easily over my body, and behind the starry cut-outs was a glimpse of tantalising pale flesh. Firm, pale flesh.

Giddy with pride and delight, I'd swept my hair up and secured it with a couple of diamanté combs, then added the glorious earrings, which swung like trophies.

"We're waiting, Alice, dear," Mum's voice had wafted up the stairs.

Obviously they'd decided I'd earned my moment of glory and deserved all the attention which was about to be flung in my direction.

"Just coming," I'd called back, sliding my feet into the high-heeled silver sandals.

"Oh, no," I'd wailed, realising suddenly that my feet had also lost weight.

Instead of fitting beautifully and making me feel like I was walking on air, my perfect accessories had now taken on the proportions of Dad's carpet slippers.

"Alice?" Mum's voice again, only louder this time.

There had been no alternative, nothing else in my wardrobe which would do. Clenching my toes, I'd purposefully made my way down the stairs as if I'd been on the Paris catwalk.

Gran's "My Goodness!" had just reached my ears when it happened . . .

SO here I am . . . waiting for Jamie. He's been an absolute angel, visiting me every single one of the seven days I've spent in hospital, sometimes twice, bringing enormous boxes of hazelnut chocolates and litres of cola.

I need "feeding up", he's told me.

And Serena, the assistant in the boutique where I'd bought the dress, has turned up trumps, too.

Seeing something she really fancied in the window, Mum had called in, and in course of the conversation had revealed how I'd taken a really nasty tumble down the stairs.

"How absolutely dreadful," Serena had said, sounding, according to Mum, as if it were all her fault, then she'd turned up on the doorstep with a selection of gorgeous stuff for me to try.

"Goodness, you have lost weight," she'd said, earning my eternal devotion. Even more so when she'd offered me a large discount on the floaty chiffon outfit I'd turned my nose up at originally, and which really does make my eyes look an incredible shade of hazel brown.

For good measure she'd loaned me a pretty matching necklace and a 20s-style beaded bag. Then she'd offered me a refund on the dress.

But there's no way on earth I could even consider parting with it. Right now, it's nestling under layers of tissue, just waiting to make its proper debut.

It's still the most perfectly-wonderful piece of clothing I've ever owned and, anyway, I've got a honeymoon coming up in the not-too-distant future.

Plenty of time to get back into shape . . ■

The Twilight Hours

by Marian Hipwell

They had an uncanny way of bringing even the deepest of secrets out into the light . . .

WITH my best wishes to you and your wife for the festive season, Bill. Same as always."

"How very kind, Hazel. And for you —" Bill Marston rummaged in the shelf below his counter "— with our regards, and we hope you enjoy it."

"Enjoy it? Christmas wouldn't be the same without Alice's cake!" Hazel took the parcel from him. "My thanks to you both."

The same old ritual had been going on for some years now. Bill, the night porter, would give her a Christmas cake baked by his wife, and in exchange Hazel always presented him with a large box of chocolates.

The cake was up to Alice's usual high standard. Rich, moist, beautifully iced — and lethal to Hazel's digestion. And, since she lived on her own and had no family to share it with, she would do what she always did and quietly find a good worthy cause to donate it to.

Stowing her outer clothes away in her cubby hole, she went in search of her floor polisher.

She'd been cleaning this office block for more years than she cared to remember and hoped to be doing so for a while longer. The evening hours suited her fine.

Here and there, an occasional light burned as people worked late in order to ease their workload so they could get away early the following day, on Christmas Eve.

At last, there was just the main office left to do and then it was time for home.

Leaving her polisher, Hazel pushed open the door and looked round. The room was in darkness, but from the adjoining office a sliver of light could be seen. No doubt it would be Miss Pym.

She was an odd one, all right, Hazel mused. She'd been here three years now, and though she didn't say much on the subject, it was well-known that she wasn't liked by her staff — you didn't have to be a genius to know that.

Some of the comments she heard as the office staff passed her on her way in at night were far from flattering.

The young girls were the worst, of course. Yet in spite of everything, Hazel couldn't help feeling that Miss Pym wasn't as bad as they made her out to be.

HAZEL made her way across the darkened room. She'd just pop her head around the door, to let Miss Pym know she was around, so she wouldn't be startled by the noise of the machine.

But as she neared the door Hazel realised it wasn't closed and she could make out the sound of a woman's soft, quiet weeping.

Miss Pym — crying? Surely not?

"Who's there?" Miss Pym's voice didn't have its usual briskness and austerity. Instead it was muffled and anxious, and it stopped Hazel in her tracks.

"Only me, Miss Pym," she answered matter-of-factly. "Just about to start cleaning the general office."

The other woman appeared at the door. Hazel could see the streaks on her face where she'd wiped her tears hurriedly. Her hair, normally neat to the point of severity, looked somewhat bedraggled and untidy.

Seeing her, Hazel's expression softened immediately.

"Bad day, Miss Pym?" Hazel asked in a sympathetic tone.

Tears welled up again in the other woman's eyes.

"What is it, love?"

Concerned, Hazel forgot herself enough to walk towards the other woman and place a comforting hand on her arm.

"Oh, nothing. Please, don't worry." Miss Pym was making a valiant attempt at recovering herself. "I've a bit of a cold, you see."

Hazel nodded. What had she been thinking of, anyway? Miss Pym was an office supervisor and she was merely a cleaning lady. Hardly the sort of person she'd choose to confide in.

Yet the wretchedness in the other woman's eyes tore at Hazel's heartstrings.

"All set for Christmas then?" She couldn't think of a single decent thing to say to ease the intense awkwardness of the situation.

"Yes. Well, I'll be celebrating on my own, as usual.You're on your own, too, aren't you, Hazel?"

"Afraid so. Ever since my husband died. Not that I mind too much, so long as I've got the television."

"Well, I mustn't keep you from your work." The usual brisk, controlled tone was once again returning to Miss Pym's voice.

"Right," Hazel said firmly. "Well, let me know if there's anything — well . . . just anything."

Miss Pym had certainly regained her composure now, yet that desperately sad look still lingered hauntingly in her eyes.

"And don't work too long, now," Hazel added sternly. "Get off home . . ."

Miss Pym stared at her in surprise. "You know, you're the first person who's ever said anything like that to me. Most people here wouldn't care if I worked myself to the bone all night," she said quietly. "In fact, I know they'd prefer it if I did so that I didn't come here in the day time."

Hazel stared at her disbelievingly. It was so unlike the younger woman to unburden herself like this. Yet she'd found that happening quite frequently on her rounds.

Evening seemed to bring out a different side to people and made them talk in a different vein from the way they would in the daytime. The twilight hours had an uncanny way of loosening tongues.

"Come on, now — we can't have you feeling sorry for yourself," Hazel said gruffly. "Girls been giving you a rough time today, have they?"

"You're right, on both counts," Miss Pym said, sighing. "They've been giving me a difficult time and, no, I shouldn't be giving in so easily to self pity like this. It must be Christmas bringing it on."

Yes, this time of year had a knack of doing that to a person, Hazel agreed silently.

She should have thought of something cheerfully non-committal to say, gone on her way, then put the whole episode to the back of her mind. Yet, she lingered.

"Come and have a brew with me," she said impulsively.

But immediately after finishing the sentence she regretted the offer. It was completely out of place, and made on the spur of the moment in a misguided attempt to chase that piteous look away from the other woman's eyes.

Miss Pym would refuse, she thought.

"Thanks, I will," Miss Pym seemed surprised herself by her immediate response.

"Right." Hazel injected some enthusiasm into her voice. "Come on, then."

ISN'T this nice and cosy?" Miss Pym commented as she followed Hazel into her cubby hole.

"There you are." Hazel handed her unexpected guest a steaming cup of tea. "There's a drop of something in it to keep the cold out, too. Just a drop, mind. It'll bring new heart into you — wait and see."

"I doubt it." The other woman spoke quietly, almost matter-of-factly. "In fact, I've lost so much heart that I'm seriously thinking of resigning."

"Oh, it's never that bad!" Hazel protested, shocked at the woman's frank admission.

"Isn't it? It's a good job, and I run the office efficiently — I know that. But it is too much to expect to be liked as well?"

Hazel looked at her, wondering if more tears were on their way. And as she looked, she noticed that Miss Pym's eyes, though dry, held a hopelessness which was far more heart-rending to see.

"Bosses are never popular," Hazel said consolingly.

"But hated?" Miss Pym asked.

"I doubt if anyone hates you," Hazel insisted.

"Miss Prim, one of the girls calls me. She doesn't know I know, of course. I overheard her one day. And she's right, I suppose. I am prim — and proper — and staid and old and ugly."

Hazel put down her cup abruptly. "If you're old, I'm Methuselah," she exclaimed, "and as for prim and proper, that's not such a bad thing to be in this modern world. And any young lass will say that of a woman she has to buckle under to."

"I didn't deliberately avoid marriage, you know," Miss Pym mused. "But I didn't mind not marrying, either. I was satisfied with my career, you see."

"Those lasses —" Hazel eyed the other woman thoughtfully "— have you ever tried to see their side of things?"

"Oh, yes." Miss Pym gave a bitter laugh. "I've often looked at myself and seen what they see. But I have to get on to them. If I don't, they won't work — particularly at this time of year."

"They're just excited and looking forward to the break," Hazel said. "You can't expect the same workload from them. Not until after Christmas, anyway."

"They bought each other presents today." Miss Pym's voice wavered suddenly. "I saw them exchanging them. Not one of them thought of bringing something in for me."

"Did you bring something in for them?" Hazel countered.

"Well, I had one or two small things in my desk, just in case . . . But —" She shrugged. "— I'd just embarrass them, anyway."

"Perhaps not," Hazel said. She pursed her lips. "Try it and see what happens."

"Oh, I couldn't." Miss Pym looked at her in alarm. "Besides, they'd think I was trying to buy their friendship or something."

"Nonsense," Hazel said. "As a matter of fact, I've something for you. That's partly why I brought you here, to give it to you. And I'm not trying to buy your friendship, am I?"

She hadn't intended saying that, but she'd had an inspirational idea. She didn't really have anything for the other woman — well, nothing bought specially.

"Merry Christmas, Miss Pym." Hazel smiled as she handed the Christmas cake to her.

Opening it, the other woman stared at it. "And it's home baked, too. How kind of you."

Hazel hastily suppressed a twinge of conscience.

"It's so big," Miss Pym went on. "I'll never eat it all. And I'm on a diet — oh, what am I saying?" She shook her head. "It looks delicious. And I'll be hanged if I'll diet over Christmas!"

"That's the spirit." Hazel eyed her

speculatively. "You could do something else with it, you know."

"Oh?" The other woman looked at her quizzically.

"You could cut it up and share it round the office tomorrow. And perhaps I might suggest a small glass of sherry to accompany it?"

"Oh, but I couldn't!"

"You could," Hazel said. "If you wanted things to change, it would be a good place to start."

Miss Pym sat immersed in thought for a few seconds.

"Sherry?" she asked at last. "During office hours?"

"A tot won't do any harm," Hazel murmured. "I doubt if anyone will mind at this time of year. Then you could distribute those little packages you have in your desk and tell them it's a thank you for all they've done throughout the year.

"You never know, you might even get more work out of them next year," she added.

Miss Pym's face broke into a genuine smile.

"I think I might just take your advice. Would you come in and have a slice with us, Hazel?"

"Well, if I can manage. It's busy you know, my first hour, but I'll do my best to get in as soon as I can."

★★★★

But with it being Christmas Eve and the streets thronged with last-minute shoppers, the journey to work took even longer than normal.

When she did finally arrive, she paused outside the door of the general office to listen for a moment.

There was plenty of laughter and among it she recognised Miss Pym's.

Pushing open the door a little, she peered in to see some sort of party going on.

Miss Pym was dressed as severely as ever but her hair was different, softer, untidier. In all the festivities someone had even put a paper hat on her head.

She was sitting happily among her staff, smiling, and the flush on her face didn't look entirely due to the sherry she was dispensing with such generosity.

And then she saw the chocolates she'd given to Bill, the night porter, lying on the table next to the remains of the cake. She couldn't help but smile.

So she wasn't the only one who'd been looking for good causes at this time of year.

And in Miss Pym, it seemed they couldn't have found a better one . . . ■

Maybe she and her handsome neighbour didn't squabble often — but their pets did!

Like Cat And Dog!

by Isobel Stewart

L UCY checked the tea-tray as the removal van next door drove away. Teapot, milk, sugar, and a plate of home-made biscuits. A nice neighbourly gesture, she told herself.

The fact that her new neighbour was male, six feet tall, and really nice looking, had nothing at all to do with it!

"Won't be long," she told her mongrel, William, jauntily.

William eased his large black frame into a comfortable position in the doorway and watched as she went down the path.

The small cottage in which she lived was one of a long row, each one cosily clinging to the next.

Lucy rang next-door's bell.

"Hi," she said brightly when the door opened. "I'm your neighbour on the right — thought you might be glad of a cup of tea."

"You must be psychic." He waved a hand to the tiny hall, and the boxes that almost reached the ceiling. I doubt if I'll ever find my kettle again!"

She held out the tray to him. "I'll leave you to get on with things — I'm Lucy Baynes."

"Well, it's nice having you for a neighbour, Lucy," he said. "I'm Rob Wilson. Maybe once I'm settled we could —"

He stopped. "Good grief!" he said.

Lucy looked round. William had managed to paw the front door open and was coming to tell her how clever he was.

"William!" she said sternly.

"He's yours, this . . . er, dog?" her neighbour asked, a little faintly.

William sat down on Lucy's foot and looked up at his mistress adoringly, his face creasing into a doggy version of a grin.

"Look!" Lucy pointed out proudly. "He's smiling."

"Is he?" Rob swallowed. I only hope —"

But what he only hoped remained unsaid. For in one fluid movement, William bounded past Rob Wilson.

Lucy closed her eyes. This wasn't happening. Without waiting to be invited, she followed William through the narrow hallway, into the tiny living-room.

It was full of piled-up furniture and packing cases, and right on top of the highest pile sat a very angry fluffy tabby cat.

"William!" Lucy shouted. "Come here!"

"I'm sorry." She turned to face her new neighbour.

He looked furious. "Would you mind getting that — thing — out of here before he does any more damage."

A LITTLE later, Lucy's doorbell rang. It was Rob Wilson. "Thank you for the tea," he said stiffly and held out the tray.

"That's OK," Lucy replied, equally stiffly. "I'm sorry William chased your cat. He never catches them," she explained. "He just likes the chase."

"That was pretty obvious," Rob Wilson returned frostily. "I just hope the experience doesn't make Oliver run away from his new home."

But Oliver didn't run away.

He took to sitting on the wall between the two houses, a wall that was just too high for William to jump over. He would sit there, grooming himself, yawning in the winter sunshine and narrowing his eyes smugly at William.

William, who had hitherto adapted to life in a small cottage with a tiny garden extremely well, began to behave very badly.

Old Mrs Brown very apologetically told Lucy that William had been barking so much that she'd had to turn her television up, and Captain Forbes in Number Eleven told her William's barking had stopped him from getting a wink of sleep in the afternoon.

Lucy apologised to both of them.

Usually she left the kitchen door ajar so that William could go in and out as he liked. She told William the next day, "If I hear that you've been barking today, that's it. No more open doors."

WHEN she got home from work, Lucy was surprised not to find William there to greet her when she unlocked the front door. He seemed to know when she was due back and would usually bring her a present — a shoe or a washing-up glove — as a token of his appreciation. But today — nothing.

Lucy went through the house and out the open kitchen door.

William was sitting at the foot of the very tall old oak tree.

"Inside, William!" she ordered.

With a martyred look and ears and tail down, William plodded away from the tree and into the kitchen.

Lucy closed the door behind him and walked down the short garden path to the tree. Oliver's outraged face peered down at her, and she could see the tip of his tail swishing irritably.

She said, "Nice puss. Nice Oliver. Come here."

Oliver, though, stayed where he was. Lucy went back into the kitchen and opened a tin of salmon.

"Puss, puss — Oliver — see what I've got for you," she said, as she came back into the garden with her offerings. Oliver didn't budge.

"He doesn't like tuna." Rob Wilson's voice was cool and amused from the other side of the wall.

Lucy swung round.

"It isn't tuna. It's salmon," she snapped.

He smiled. "Don't worry about Oliver. He'll come down when he's good and ready, as long as that monster isn't waiting for him."

Lucy drew herself to her full five-foot four and glared at him.

"Perhaps," she said, "you'd be good enough to inform me when my dog can go back out into his own garden again!"

FOR two days Lucy kept William shut in the house while she was at work. Then she asked herself why she and William should have to change their way of life because of a new arrival.

"We were here first," she told William the next morning, as she opened up the kitchen door. "But for heavens' sake, just ignore the cat!"

Unfortunately, when she got home, it was all too clear that William hadn't ignored Oliver. There was a big scratch down his face.

Lucy knelt down on the doormat and put her arms around him.

He moaned pitifully, and held up a completely uninjured paw for her to see.

"What's wrong with him?" Rob Wilson said, as he went into his cottage.

Silently, Lucy pointed to the scratch on William's face.

"Is Oliver all right?" she asked in a small voice.

"Oh, yes. Actually, I think we just have to let the two of them sort things out for themselves."

Lucy closed the door firmly. Rob was right about William and Oliver. They would just have to sort things out.

ONE of William's great pleasures in life was his final inspection of his territory just before bedtime every night. Lucy would open the door, William would walk out, and then, in a leisurely fashion, he would walk up and down the pavement until he was satisfied everything was as it should be.

Sometimes, though, his leisurely fashion was just a little too leisurely.

"Come along, William," Lucy said impatiently. She was already bathed and in her Mickey Mouse nightie, and the sharp February air was not at all conducive to a long wait.

She went out for him and grabbed his collar.

Suddenly, the wind caught the door and it shut — and locked — behind her. Lucy shivered. It was freezing, and there was no way she could get into her house.

There was only one thing she could do.

Lucy grasped William's collar tightly and walked down Rob Wilson's path. At least there was still a light on.

Her neighbour opened the door.

"Lucy?" he said, astonished. "It's . . . er . . . a bit late for visiting, surely?" She could see him fighting not to laugh.

"I've locked myself out," Lucy said stiffly. "I wondered if I could climb over your wall — my back door's open."

William, the traitor, was greeting Rob effusively and

enthusiastically. Absently, Rob scratched the big dog's ears.

"Sure — come in," he said. "You look cold."

Lucy was all too conscious of her Mickey Mouse nightie.

"I am," she said shortly, and followed him into the house.

Rob stepped into what she knew must be his bedroom.

"Here," he said, handing her a dressing-gown, "you'd better put this on."

"Thank you," Lucy replied. "Maybe you'd better hold William while I climb over the wall, if you don't mind."

"I've just made cocoa. Why don't you have a cup first?"

"I don't know . . ." Lucy began.

He smiled that winning smile and champagne corks popped in Lucy's head.

It was only when she was sitting on a stool in the tiny kitchen, watching Rob pour two mugs of cocoa, that she thought of William.

"William!" she said. "And Oliver!"

Rob's hand was large and warm and reassuring on hers.

"I told you they'd have to sort things out," he said. He took her hand. "Let's go and see how they're doing. I'm sure if they were fighting, we'd know about it."

William was sitting in the middle of the room. Oliver was on the table. Cautiously, William moved a little closer. Oliver sat still, watching him, then jumped off the table and strolled over.

Lucy held her breath. She realised that Rob's arm was around her shoulder — and she rather liked it being there.

Oliver looked at William. William looked back. Oliver lifted one paw, and then, with his claws sheathed, he gave William a tap on the nose.

"Just making a point," Rob whispered, his lips against Lucy's ear.

Oliver, obviously feeling he didn't want to push his luck, strolled back across to the safety of the table. William, the strain too much for him, ran to Lucy and wound his large black paws round her legs.

"It's all right, you're a very good boy," she told him.

"You certainly are," Rob added and he patted William, too.

"Not bad for a start?" he said.

"Not at all bad," Lucy agreed. She was pretty sure that Rob wasn't just talking about William and Oliver.

"I'll climb over the wall," Rob offered, "and let you and William in."

"You don't have to do that," Lucy protested.

"Well," he laughed. "That's what neighbours are for — to be neighbourly."

Friends and neighbours, she thought. It sounded good. In fact, some day, with a bit of luck, they might become much more than that. ∎

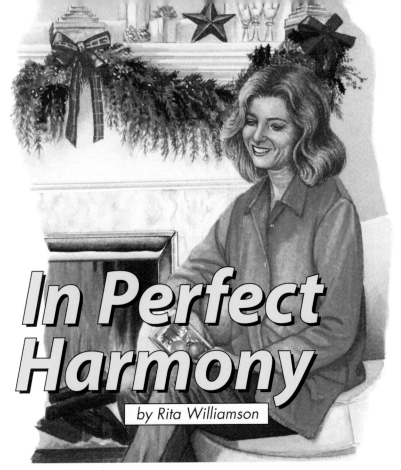

In Perfect Harmony

by Rita Williamson

She thought all the fun had gone out of the festive season — until an unlikely partner put a song back in her heart!

A ND a Merry Christmas to you, too, you vicious thing!" Violet May Johns, postwoman to the village of Ardenly, snapped unseasonally at the wicked letter-box that had trapped the fingers of her black, woolly glove.

Violet reclaimed her glove from the possessive letter-box and slipped her chilly fingers back into the protective warmth. She turned on her heel and retreated along the path, whistling a wry little Gilbert and Sullivan parody that, "a postlady's lot is not a happy one".

She slammed the iron gate shut and enjoyed the piercing clanging tones that echoed throughout the cul-de-sac. As she did so, she uttered a caustic comment upon the festive season.

"Pah, Christmas!"

There was a time when Violet used to really enjoy Christmas and everything that went with it; carols and laughter, mistletoe and holly, angels and tinsel. The whole festive set-up never failed to bring warmth and hope to her heart.

But those memories were embedded deep in the past, and, five brief years ago, had taken on a whole new meaning. It had been this very time of year when her beloved Harry had died.

Christmas, so painfully and horribly bleak that year, had been cruelly and irreparably tainted ever since.

But for Violet, the trauma didn't end there — much worse was to come. As if losing a husband of 35 years hadn't been enough, she'd also discovered, to her horror, that the money coming in no longer paid the bills. So, as a necessity and an anchor in the world of confusion, Violet found herself a job as a postwoman.

★★★★

When Harry had been alive, Christmas had been the most wonderful, joyous time of the year.

To Violet, December was one long, happy round of baking as she churned out mince pies and sausage rolls in abundance for the many friends and colleagues Harry invited in. The life and soul of the party — that was her Harry.

IT was 7.30 on a dismal Monday morning the week before Christmas. Clouds, heavy with snow, hung in the sky and delayed the dawn. Violet noticed that the day was as grey and dark as her mood.

She flicked quickly through the pile of cards for Number 22, amazed that Miss Enderby's past pupils still remembered her. Year in, year out, the retired teacher was swamped with greetings cards.

Today, like every other, in her usual early-morning fashion, Violet began to sing a little song.

This morning, part of her wanted to sing something low and mournful, but instead she chose a tune that would cheer her up — one of Harry's favourites.

The happy song did the trick and by the time she'd pedalled to Number 46, her usual good humour had almost returned. Violet parked her bike and took a parcel out of her sack.

This'll never go through the box, she mused. I just hope they're awake. She rang the doorbell and waited. After what seemed like an eternity, she rang again and a voice could be heard coming closer.

"All right, all right. I'm coming!" The door opened ever so slightly and a dishevelled head peered grumpily around the edge. Violet held out the parcel as if in offering. A thin arm reached out and grabbed it. "You could have left it on the doorstep . . ."

166

Violet could have launched into a spiel about the rules and regulations of taking unclaimed mail back to the post office, but she didn't. She simply said, "But it's too wet."

And with that the door closed instantly and abruptly.

Well! As she heaved herself back on to her bicycle, she mused for a moment on what the Three Kings might have felt had Mary come to the stable door and uttered the words — "You could've left the parcels on the doorstep!"

AT Number 78, Tibbles the cat was rudely awakened from her cosy slumber under the radiator by a shower of mail. Tibbles stalked away from the offending letters with an air of affront.

And Violet adopted much the same air as she returned to her bicycle.

As she pedalled away, she sang about Good King Wenceslas and began to commiserate with the lonely peasant who'd been gathering fuel.

She muttered to herself and sighed. "Just call me Scrooge! I'm even fed up with Christmas . . ."

"Well, hello, Scrooge!"

The deep male voice belonged to Stanley Blythe, the village milkman.

Violet responded somewhat shyly, feeling rather silly after being caught talking to herself.

"Oh, good morning, Stan."

"You were talking to yourself again, weren't you, Violet?"

She smiled at him. "Well, at least I don't get any backchat . . ."

He acknowledged the wisdom of her statement with a smile. "So what's made my lovely Violet turn into an old Scrooge, then?"

Violet was a little shocked to be referred to as his "lovely Violet", but the pleasure of it made her smile broadly and she felt more like her old self again. Suddenly she forgot all about her bad mood and the world seemed full of tinsel and mistletoe.

SHE free-wheeled her bike down the slope to the flats at Chambers Court. The small car park was covered with an even carpet of clean white snow. No-one had stirred yet and Violet experienced an almost childish, forbidden pleasure in making a large figure-of-eight in the pristine surface with her tyre tracks.

By the time she'd hauled herself to the top floor of the last block of flats, her singing had faded to little more than a breathless hum.

She slipped a thick pile of cards through the door of Number 12. The owner was a pretty young girl who received stacks of mail.

Probably love letters, Violet thought smilingly. She felt a little like Cupid and wondered whether wings on her heels might be more appropriate than a battered old bicycle.

The next delivery was for young Mr Perry at Number 8. From the pile of official-looking letters he received, Violet guessed he was job-hunting. She was sad to think she could be the bearer of so many hurtful rejection letters.

Just as she was about to tackle the letter-box, the door burst open.

"Merry Christmas, Violet!" Young Mr Perry bounced forward, placed a kiss on her cheek, and thrust a gaily-coloured package at her.

"What on earth?"

Jason Perry smiled warmly at her. "Merry Christmas, Violet. That's just a little token of my great appreciation. You're the very best postlady there is, you know."

"I am?" she uttered blankly, still staring disbelievingly at the little gift.

Young Mr Perry nodded firmly. "Day in, day out, you troop up here with my letters, and you're always singing. No matter what day of the week, whatever the weather, you always have a lovely song for me."

Violet blushed, feeling suddenly very shy and vulnerable knowing that so many people listened to her tuneful renditions.

"You don't know how many times you've cheered me up," he continued, "so I thought it was about time I returned the favour. Merry Christmas."

Violet couldn't take her eyes off the lovely little parcel in her hands.

"Thank you, Mr Perry, and Merry Christmas to you."

She thought a moment about her earlier judgment on the season and decided she'd been proved wrong. Very wrong, in fact. Christmas was still Christmas and nobody could alter that fact.

Although conscious of the noise she generated in the echoing stairwell, she couldn't contain the happiness and goodwill in her heart, and before she knew it, she was singing a happy tune again.

"Hark the herald angels sing, glory to the new-born King . . ."

The rolling sound of the carol echoed around the stairwell and Violet sang deeply and with passion. As she reached the middle landing, she could hear a young, happy voice above her, *"Peace on Earth and mercy mild, God and sinners reconciled . . ."*

She was beaming broadly as she passed Stan, the milkman, who was singing as he made his way through the entrance hall.

"Merry Christmas, Stan!"

"That's much better!" he declared. "Now you sound as though you mean it!"

"Well, Stan, I really think I do this time."

As she checked her bag for forgotten letters, she found herself entranced with Stan's deep, melodious tones, and instead of pedalling back to the post office, she waited for him to return to his float.

She didn't like to analyse why she did it, but she guessed it was something to do with the mistletoe and Christmas spirit.

When Stan finally reappeared, she was almost at a loss for something to say.

"You have a fine voice, Stan," she uttered at last.

"Well, with a father from the Welsh Valleys, it's only to be expected.

"You have a lovely voice yourself, Violet. You're always singing, and I must admit you've brightened many a morning for me . . ."

She blushed and felt suddenly very shy.

There was an awkward silence between them, then Stan said, "Would you like to come to the carol concert tomorrow night, Violet?"

Violet was both astonished and thrilled by his tentative enquiry. She stared at him as though seeing him for the first time, and realised that he really was a handsome man.

Violet felt her heart beat ten to the dozen.

"Yes, Stan, I'd love to, really love to. Thanks for asking."

She was delighted to see pleasure and relief cross his face at her reply. Well, who'd have thought Stan was such a shy old thing? She flushed with all the excitement and felt a very early spring in the air.

"I thought it'd be nice to sing something together . . ." he said.

Violet felt just like a teenager in the first throes of passion. "Come on, then . . ."

So the residents of Chambers Court were treated to the sound of their milkman and postlady singing, arm in arm, in the snow-covered car park.

And if Violet sang any more carols that morning, it was through force of habit, for her mind was busy on other things, like what to wear to the carol concert, and whether she'd have time to make some of her special mince pies, maybe even a sausage roll or two.

After all, it would only be right to invite Stan back for a little sherry and some Christmas fare.

And pedalling slowly down the High Street, Violet May Johns felt happy and contented in the knowledge that Christmas was, indeed, the very best time of the year. ■

Our Country-Lane Years

By June M. Hodges

Those sunkissed, pony-trekking days belonged to yesterday. Yet I was finding it difficult — impossible — to let them go . . .

GET those muddy boots off my carpet!" The words came back to me now across the years, echoing in the empty house, along with a host of warm memories that shimmered before my eyes.

How I longed for those muddy boots now. But there was only silence — no happy jangle of voices, no deafening din, no laughter.

I stood at the window and watched the heavy rain sweeping across the valley.

It was nine o'clock on a Monday morning and I was alone — and sad.

I had at last been given back my life — and found it to be empty and meaningless.

I was 43, overweight and rather plain, with no real skills except cooking, washing and cleaning.

And just being there for everybody, of course.

The rain was easing off, so I decided to go for a walk.

When I reached the field, Captain, Beth's horse, snorted and wandered across to me.

"Well, boy, it's just you and me now. Both of us redundant and unwanted!"

I touched his velvet nose and his lips brushed my hand. He'd been a dream once, a childhood dream — Beth's and mine — but mostly mine.

My parents hadn't been able to afford to buy me my own horse, so

I'd muddled along learning to ride on friends' ponies, having the occasional lesson at a riding school, and spending most of my time gazing over gates with a desperate, fierce longing.

And then I grew up and had my children, but the dream never died. It grew with me, and was born again in Beth, my daughter.

And so, I was determined that Beth would have what I never could.

I did all sorts of jobs — typing from home, market research, cleaning — anything, in fact, to save enough money.

We rented some land a mile or so away and eventually Captain came into our lives.

They were the special years: the carefree, cuddling, country-lane years.

We shared Captain, and were like sisters — until Beth grew up and went forward into her bright, golden future, and left us behind, me and Captain.

She'd finally left me, left home, last Sunday, when we took her by car to university, and my loss was complete.

Hugh, my husband, was very philosophical about it, but then men are. Besides, he had his own hobbies, his job and his colleagues.

He had a life. I had nothing — only poor, unwanted Captain, who would now fall out of condition because I was too heavy to ride him.

Now here we were, he and I, in limbo, on a wet Monday morning, set adrift on a lonely, endless sea with our anchor gone.

I moped about all day.

Then, the next morning, I got up, looked in the mirror at my bleak, flabby features — and went into town to find the rest of my life.

I registered at the Job Centre and scanned the situations vacant.

On the way home, I bought a calorie-counting book, and sat down to plan menus accordingly. The search for the new me had begun!

BETH came home after three weeks for the weekend. "Gosh, Mum, you look different . . ."

Already, I'd lost a few pounds and had been for a couple of interviews. I was beginning to feel better, more assertive.

Then she said the words I had secretly been dreading.

"Um . . . I've been thinking. I could do with some extra money, Mum. You know, for books and clothes and stuff. Perhaps it's time we found a good home for Captain?"

She dropped her eyes, and I felt a great sadness come down over the golden afternoon.

I knew she was right. It wasn't fair to keep him now, vegetating and eating his head off. He was getting fat and would eventually become ill through lack of exercise.

"OK, we'll cobble an advert together after tea," I said bleakly.

I started my new job for a car sales company soon after that weekend.

I was rusty to say the least. My last memory of an office was a flashing switchboard that squawked like a whooper swan, and a typewriter like a battleship in full sail. Still, I was eager to learn, and slowly, very slowly, I began to enjoy myself. It was almost an adventure. As I grew slimmer, I grew more confident. I bought new clothes, had my hair cut, and even took a beginners' course on computers.

The world was my oyster, and Alan Ingrams, my boss, was the pearl in it. He was kind, patient, considerate, extremely attractive — and extremely married!

Then the warning bells began to sound. I was entering a danger zone, a minefield.

But I was in it before I could look where my great big feet were going.

MEANWHILE, back at the ranch, poor old Hugh was concerned, to say the least. He was visibly disturbed at the change in me, while I couldn't help but chuckle that it was about time, too!

He had taken me for granted, wrapped up in his own little world, while I slaved over two lively children and a herbaceous border.

When Beth came home for Christmas, I overheard him asking her, "Do you think your mother's all right? She's so different. You don't think, well, you know . . ."

Beth sounded surprised. "Know what, Dad?"

"Well, it's as if . . . Oh, Beth, come on, I can talk to you as an adult now, can't I?"

"As if she's got another man, you mean?" Beth asked.

"Well, yes, if you like . . ."

I smiled, but, at the same time, I felt something catch at my heart and a little voice somewhere deep inside warned, "Watch it!"

"Well, it would serve you right if she has," Beth quipped. "It's about time she had a life."

Beth cornered me later that night and began interrogating me. Not about my suspect affair, but about Captain.

"Mum, I know this isn't easy for you. It isn't easy for me, either. I love Captain, too, but I need the money. Has anyone been to see him yet?"

Yes, they had, unfortunately.

There had been a horrible, shifty, greasy character called Potter who'd posed as a family man wanting a pony for his children. He'd smelled of dealers' yards and dirty deals.

Then there had been the Conolly-Carews and their daughter,

Caroline. They'd arrived in a Range-Rover, both mother and daughter wearing matching suede culottes.

Poor Captain had ambled towards us looking very fat and tatty, his mane straggly and unkempt and rubbing himself on a tree.

Daddy had looked down his nose and Caroline had looked bored.

I'd got my tuppence worth in before they did. "Look, I'm very sorry, but I don't think you're what we're looking for . . ."

So, yes, I had made an effort, I pointed out to Beth.

But, no, I hadn't found anyone worthy of our dear old friend.

Captain needed love and affection, care and time. He needed people like us.

SO the long summer days at the office passed. Hot, sweltering, fan-humming, bare-leg days, when the forecourt, full of shiny cars, shimmered.

And there were those long, sultry evenings of working late, then escaping to leafy, breeze-kissed lanes, stopping at a country pub for a drink, sitting outside while the sun slid into the river; the scent of hedgerows and new-mown hay.

I was growing scared. The time was fast approaching when I would have to make a choice, a firm decision.

Then one night Hugh suddenly asked, "Have you got anything to tell me, love?"

I was startled.

"A secret perhaps?" He was calm, but his eyes betrayed his inner turmoil.

Yes, I had a secret. But I couldn't tell him, not yet. Everything was different, and I knew now what I wanted and where I was going.

"I mean, where do you go after work, when you're late?"

I couldn't resist a shadow of a smile. "I told you, Hugh. I call on Captain on the way home. After being shut in all day, I just have to get out and breathe some fresh air."

Then one weekend a family turned up and I liked them right away.

The girl was petite and gentle, and her parents were kind and caring.

She loved Captain immediately; there was an instant rapport. It forced the issue.

Beth was due home for the weekend and I knew she was having a struggle paying for her books, food and lodgings on her student loan.

I knew that a decision had to be made.

The wind was cold as we stood at the gate and talked about